CORPORATE AFFAIRS

Carrie's

ANSWER

SIERRA & VJ
SUMMERS

ELLORA'S CAVE
ROMANTICA®
www.EllorasCave.com

An Ellora's Cave Publication

www.ellorascave.com

Carrie's Answer

ISBN 9781419966163
ALL RIGHTS RESERVED.
Carrie's Answer Copyright © 2011 Sierra & VJ Summers
Edited by Carrie Jackson.
Design and Photography by Darrell King.

Electronic book publication August 2011
Trade paperback publication 2012

CARRIE'S ANSWER

Dedication

ဆ

It takes a village to write a book – Carrie's Answer is proof of that! Thanks to Lora for planting the seed, Dori for helping it grow, Deanna and Carrie for sticking with us on the learning curve, and every person who met and loved Carrie and Marcus. We hope you enjoy seeing them in a new light.

Chapter One

∞

Marcus Worthington pulled his Lexus into the parking space in front of his condo, eager to see his wife after a lengthy business trip to Chicago. In the next space, Daniel Ellis had parked his blue Aston Martin. It was Marcus' second anniversary and he wanted to surprise Karen, his adventurous wife, with a night of wild sex. Anticipation slithered up his spine as he imagined his hot wife sandwiched between him and Daniel.

He had shared Karen with his best friend twice before they were married and she had loved it. Daniel hadn't volunteered to join them again after the wedding and Marcus, completely wrapped up in his new status as a husband, hadn't asked. He'd been completely surprised when Karen had brought up the idea last week as he prepared to leave for Chicago.

It had taken some fast talking to convince Daniel to go along with it. Daniel didn't do ménage with married couples, even if part of that couple was Marcus, with whom he'd been sharing women since college. For all of his liberal views on sex, Daniel's stance on marital fidelity seemed odd to some, but Marcus understood. With all the shit that had gone down between Dan's parents, it made sense that he didn't want to participate in adultery, even when he was invited.

Marcus grabbed a bouquet of roses from the passenger seat. Karen insisted on blood-red roses. She'd laughingly told him that if he couldn't pony up the cash for her favorite blooms, not to bother with flowers at all.

He adored his wife. She was smart, classy and sexy as hell. Tall, almost six feet in height, her body was long and willowy. She'd modeled while attending law school. Her body was perfection wrapped in tanned, toned flesh. She worked out more than most men and commanded attention wherever she went.

Marcus had taken a lot of shit from his friends and family when he'd married her. They thought she was cold. They thought she was a witch. His siblings Matthew and Meri had even taken to calling her "The Viper". Marcus knew they just didn't understand her.

He understood her better than anyone. On the outside she was tough, maybe even a little bit brittle. As one of the premiere defense attorneys in Detroit, she had to be. She took control of the audience whenever a camera and microphone pointed in her direction. She won case after case and even had firms from New York and Los Angeles fighting to give her partnerships.

But when they were alone, she was all warm, willing woman.

When they were alone, her tough public persona slid away like a mist. She was attentive, fawning all over him. She gave him almost anything he asked for. And the things she wouldn't, well they weren't really that important. He was happy. He'd be greedy to ask for more.

Marcus started to put his key in the door but it was slightly ajar. He pushed it open to hear Karen's voice drift from the living room, low and sexy.

"Come on, Daniel, he won't be home for another hour. Traffic from Metro is backed up all along Ninety-four."

"I'm leaving, Karen." Daniel sounded pissed. "You are one crazy bitch."

Marcus started forward, ready to defend his wife, but her next words stopped him dead.

"When he gets here, he is going to want to tie me up and I can't stand that stuff. God, I can barely stand it when he touches me anymore."

"You knew what Marcus was like when you married him. He was honest with you about his sex life from the beginning."

Her shrill laughter filled the air. "Oh please, Daniel. Do you think he really expected a woman like me to deal with that for any period of time? He wants a possession. But Marcus doesn't own me, I own *him*."

The bottom dropped out of Marcus' world as she continued her venomous rant.

"He's one of the wealthiest men in the state. Our marriage was one of convenience, not *love*. With his name attached to mine, I can work for any firm in Michigan."

"Goddamn, woman you really *are* a viper, aren't you?" Daniel's voice was deadly quiet. "If he only knew…"

"Only knew what?" Karen scoffed. "Do you think he'd believe you if you told him what happened here tonight? Do you actually think he'd believe that *I* came on to *you*? Oh, please! Which one of us is the whore here, Daniel? I'm married to Marcus. He made a commitment to me and I am committed to him. The only thing you've ever committed to is keeping the condom companies in business."

Marcus heard Daniel cross the room, moving toward the hall.

"Put your robe back on. I won't tell Marcus, only because I won't destroy him like this. But stay away from me, Karen. Stay far away."

Her laughter echoed off the pristine white walls. "Ohhh, Danny-boy, I am so afraid. Go on, get out of here. You're as pathetic as he is. Sexual deviants, both of you. Get out, Daniel. I have to take something to get me through the rest of this night."

Marcus stalked into the living room. Daniel glanced up, giving him a look of sympathy he didn't fucking want. Karen was tying the belt of her black silk robe. She smiled at Marcus.

"Baby! You're home." She sauntered over to him on four-inch stilettos. Wrapping her red-tipped fingers around his neck, she placed a loud kiss on his cheek. "Daniel and I were just discussing you."

A fury unlike any he'd ever known engulfed his body. His stomach churned, acid burning his throat. He pushed her off him and walked past her down the hall.

"Ah..." Her soft sigh stopped him. "I guess you heard our little conversation."

Marcus didn't utter a word. He just turned slowly to face the woman he'd thought loved him.

"I think you may have misunderstood what was going on, sweetheart." She used that soft, girlish voice that had once driven him insane with lust. Now it left him cold. "Daniel got here early and wanted to start before you arrived."

Marcus staggered up to her, towering above her, his heart shattering into a thousand unmendable pieces. "I heard it all, Karen. Stop fucking lying. It belittles us both."

Her sharp intake of breath was audible a moment before her hand shot out. Marcus caught her wrist before she made contact with his face.

"This is over." He threw her hand away and turned, making his way to their bedroom.

"Oh no it's not, Marcus Worthington. If you think for one second this is over, you are crazy."

He ignored her and went into their room. Ten minutes later he walked back out, his bags packed, and went to the front door. She was in the kitchen, placing the roses he'd dropped to the floor into a crystal vase.

She inhaled their fragrant scent. "Go ahead, darling. Get drunk tonight, purge your silly anger. With your sexual background, I fail to understand why you're so upset."

"My sexual background?" Marcus repeated. "I have never cheated on you, never *wanted* to cheat on you."

Karen compressed her full red lips and shrugged her shoulders. "I never thought you would expect monogamy, Marcus. I mean, how many couples in our position really do?"

Her words began to sink in, their true meaning taking root in his brain, slicing his heart.

"I expect you back home tomorrow," she added casually. "We have the charity auction at The Whitney in the evening. Be here at eight. That should give you plenty of time to come to your senses. By then, I am sure you'll come up with an appropriate apology for ruining my anniversary."

Marcus slammed out his front door for the last time. Karen had utterly emasculated him. He felt dirty, used. He wanted to scream and rage but he wouldn't give her the satisfaction. No woman would ever get that kind of hold on him again.

Daniel stood by his car, waiting for him. Hands in his pockets, he never said a word.

Marcus walked around him to the back of the vehicle. Opening the door, he threw the duffle and garment bags he'd packed onto the seat.

Daniel held out a key as he approached. "Spare room's yours for as long as you need it. The Jack Daniel's is in the cupboard next to the fridge. Save some for me."

Marcus stood stock-still while his best friend dropped the key into his palm.

"I'm sorry. Damn, but I'm sorry. You know I would never have done anything with her." Daniel stepped back, not waiting for an answer, and slid into his car. He tore out of the parking lot with a vicious squeal of tires.

Marcus got behind the wheel of his own car and pulled out. He drove along Woodward Avenue on autopilot, stopping at a corner liquor store to purchase a bottle of tequila.

Making his way to West Jefferson and then into the Cobo Center parking garage, he headed down to the riverfront on foot. Once there, he walked mindlessly, watching the flashes of light from Windsor wink at him from across the Detroit River.

Eventually he wandered into a low-lit area and sat on a concrete bench. Thoughts swirled around in his head, faster than he could keep up.

Karen. She thought he was a fucking joke. She "put up with" his perversions to further her fucking career. Her words stabbed him in the gut over and over.

His sister had warned him on more than one occasion that Karen was wrong for him. He'd laughed at her. She was young and hadn't lived long enough to know what was right for her, much less for him.

His father Stirling had warned him too, reminding him endlessly that women were faithless and weak, and making Marcus even more determined to take Karen for his own. His father had also pushed for an ironclad prenup, and Marcus had agreed with him on that one point. But she'd easily talked him out of it the first time she let him tie her up.

It had all been there right in front of him but he'd been blinded by the longest legs that had ever wrapped around his hips. He was a fucking fool. Goddamn. Marcus hung his head and did something he hadn't done since the night his mother died — he cried.

* * * * *

Two hours later, he was all cried out, drunk and comfortably numb from head to toe. On wobbly legs, he rose from the bench. He tossed the empty tequila bottle in a nearby trash can. He stumbled over to the railing. The waters were rough from the wind and slapped up the wall, getting his shoes wet as he leaned over watching the waves rush by.

Fuck, he was tired. So damn tired. Tired of hiding who he really was. Denying himself in order to make Karen happy. He'd always thought he would be able to ease her into the lifestyle. She let him tie her up on occasion. She'd fucked him and Daniel both. He'd had high hopes that she was softening up to his more exotic tastes, though he hadn't taken her to the club, thinking it would be too much for her. He was damn happy now that he hadn't.

In the back of his mind, buried deep, he must have known that she would do this to him one day. He'd seen the look in her eyes sometimes, like she had no compassion, but he'd ignored her less-than-kind qualities.

He'd known she was cold and single-minded at work but she'd never been like that with him. Hell, she was the best actress Marcus had ever seen and he was the biggest asshole in the world for turning himself over to a woman like her, for trying to change who he was to make her happy.

He swayed out over the railing, losing his balance, watching the dark water get closer. The cold spray hit him in the face but before he could tip over the rail or back to safety, a large hand grabbed his jacket and hauled him up.

Someone whipped him around, a flashlight shone brightly in his face. Marcus squinted his eyes against what felt like the sun.

"Worthington?"

Fuck, who was that? He knew the voice but couldn't place it.

"What the hell were you trying to do, man? It's too fucking cold to take a swim tonight."

The light lowered and Marcus was able to adjust his somewhat blurry vision.

Jenner. Detective Dorian Jenner. Just fucking great.

"Let's go, man. I'll get a patrol car to take you home." Jenner put his arm around Marcus, holding him upright as they walked back toward Hart Plaza.

"No' home, Jenner, take me to Dan's. Tha's my home now," he slurred.

Dorian tightened his hold as Marcus tripped over his own feet.

"You got it, buddy." Dorian did a quick two-step as Marcus lurched to the side. "For this, I better get a bump up to platinum status at the club." His easy laugh rumbled from his throat, and for the first time in hours Marcus smiled.

"Sure man, firs' thing tomorrow I'll make the call."

"Right," Dorian agreed. "If you even remember we had this conversation."

* * * * *

Three days later, the headlines screamed: "Worthington Heir Doesn't Play Nice".

When Marcus refused to speak to Karen and banned her from all Worthington properties, she got nasty and went to the papers.

What they printed was the most outrageous pack of lies he'd ever seen. Mixing fact and fiction, the stories gave details of a sexual life they'd never had. Maybe Marcus had always dreamed of doing such things to her but Karen never allowed it. Now it was out there for public consumption.

Good 'ole Stirling, as always, was so damn supportive, lecturing him on how he should keep his secrets fucking secret.

"I expect this kind of behavior from Matthew, not you, Marcus," his father had said. "You are the face of Worthington and that face has been sullied by your actions, preying on your wife like that. Well it's your mess, clean it up. I won't help. If the company folds, it's on your head."

Stirling was a master at guilt and humiliation. Marcus had avoided most of it by being the cold, calculating businessman that his father was. He knew that was where his need for total control came from. For him, that need for control had spilled from the boardroom to the bedroom.

He was rereading the article for the tenth time when Carrie Anderson came into his office. Shaking her head, she folded the paper up and tossed it in the trash.

"Marcus, stop doing this. You're giving her what she wants." Her calm, soothing voice broke him from his self-loathing. She placed a fresh cup of coffee in front of him.

He eyed his assistant bleakly. "You knew, didn't you? What I like? What I want?"

Her soft round face pinkened as she nodded. "Yes, I knew. I overheard Karen talking a time or two."

He tried to hold back a wince. God only knew what venom Karen had spewed in Carrie's direction.

She continued in a matter-of-fact voice. "Then Daniel and Matt, well they aren't exactly discreet." She was trying to make him smile but Marcus couldn't quite manage it.

"Why are you still here?" He hated the way his normally commanding voice was barely above a whisper.

Carrie grabbed his hand, and when the physical contact of her silky skin made him jump slightly, she only tightened her hold.

"I will only say this to you once, and then we will never talk about it again. You have nothing to be ashamed of. Karen is a vindictive woman who will fight tooth and nail to make you look bad. Don't let her get to you." Her other hand came to rest on the top of his head. "You're stronger than that."

She let go and walked to the door, pausing to turn halfway around to meet his defeated gaze. "Just for the record, I read that article and I don't think you're depraved. You are a good man, Marcus Worthington."

Closing the door quietly behind her, she left Marcus alone, a small amount of warmth filling his chest for the first time in days.

He was damn lucky to have Carrie here. Her words fluttered in his head, repeating over and over again. He sipped his coffee and picked up the phone to call his lawyer. It was time to end this.

Before he could dial the number, Carrie burst back through the door. Her eyes were huge and she spoke in an unsteady voice.

"Marcus, you have to get to Harper Grace Hospital, it's your father."

Chapter Two
Five Years Later

୫୨

Marcus closed the last button on his black silk shirt, his gaze glancing over the drowsy blonde lying on the red satin sheets. She was naked, sprawled on her flat stomach. Her ass was still a delightful pink from his hand, and she was sated and silent, his personal favorite kind of woman. Marcus owned this private room in the club Velvet Ice. He occasionally allowed his lovers to stay the night if they chose, but he never did. The idea of spending the night in the same bed with one of his lovers made him nauseated.

A rustle of fabric behind him drew his attention away from the sleeping woman.

"Come on, I'm thirsty." Daniel opened the door, and Marcus followed his best friend out of the VIP suites and into the low-lit hallway.

They passed another couple going into a private room. The woman wore red leather from head to toe. She was holding a leash attached to a collar worn by a very well-known Detroit businessman. Marcus acknowledged the couple with a slight nod. The club contract stated clearly that all members' identities were confidential. To outsiders, the third-floor VIP suites were no more than a rumor. The rest of the place looked like any other high-end club, full of men and women who came to drink and dance.

Since Marcus had helped the owner bankroll Velvet Ice, his room was forever his and he would continue to play whenever he chose.

"What's wrong? You have that look on your face," Daniel asked as he opened a door that led to a winding staircase.

Marcus raised an ebony brow. "What look?"

They made their way down the stairs, which opened into the large second-story dance floor. This place was also off-limits to the general public, but for those who couldn't afford the private rooms it was the next best thing. All the tables surrounding the room were full, so Marcus led the way to the smaller bar area, away from the music and noise. Grabbing a booth in the corner, he waved the waitress over.

She nodded, already knowing what the men's drink orders were. Marcus slouched comfortably, placing an arm across the back of the booth.

His friend looked at him expectantly.

"I don't know what the hell you want me to say." He glanced up with an absent smile as the waitress slid his beer in front of him. Her perfect white teeth flashed when he slipped her a twenty. She slid her hand across the table, placing it on his. She lightly pressed his hand before taking the twenty and moving away.

Daniel watched her mile-long legs in a micro-mini leather skirt slink away on five-inch stiletto heels. "*That's* what I'm talking about. She wanted you."

Marcus grunted. "No, she wanted a big tip."

Daniel laughed. "She did everything but wear a neon sign saying *fuck me* on it."

Marcus shrugged. The waitress wasn't any different than any of the other women in the club. Nice to play with but that's all.

"See," Daniel complained. "There it is again, the fucking *look*."

"Okay, why don't you tell me what's wrong?" Marcus noticed the serious expression that settled over Daniel's face. *Uh-oh, here we go.*

"You've lost something, Marcus." His friend scooted closer. "You didn't enjoy yourself tonight. Hell, you haven't enjoyed the last few times we've shared, not like you used to."

"You enjoyed it enough for both of us," Marcus tried to joke his way out of the conversation. He wasn't up for psychoanalysis tonight.

"Bullshit. You haven't been into any of the games lately."

Marcus drained the rest of his beer. Holding up the empty bottle, he signaled for another one. "I don't know what's wrong. Work's been a bitch. I'm tired of chasing after Matt. And Meredith? Well, we don't even need to go there."

That, Daniel would understand. Matthew had always been a wild child, and Meredith had never quite recovered from the double blow of Marcus' condemnation of her budding sexuality and his own subsequent fall from grace. The memory of her tear-stained face as they'd all but dragged her out of the club still haunted Daniel.

Two more bottles of beer appeared on the table in front of them.

"You've been dealing with them for years. They haven't changed, you have."

Marcus caught the waitress by the wrist. "Scotch, double."

She winked and left.

"I'm not in the mood for this conversation. Drop the subject." Marcus exhaled. How the hell could he explain to his best friend that he was tired? The kind of tired you felt deep in your bones? His life had finally started getting back to normal, yet he was empty. Sure, fucking was great, and there was no shortage of willing submissives to play with, especially when you were wealthy.

He looked around the bar at the multitude of beautiful women dressed in their designer club wear. Smiling with capped teeth, enhanced breasts displayed to their best advantage, they were living dolls, and each and every one of them left him cold. They relieved the physical need in him, allowed him to indulge in his dominance and to release the worst of the pressure, but there were no feelings there. No connection.

Hell, to anyone else his life looked perfect. CEO of one of the most prosperous businesses in the Midwest, single, rich, but it wasn't enough for him anymore. God, he felt like such a sap but all he wanted was a woman who didn't desire anything more from him than to submit. To allow him to give her more pleasure than she ever knew she wanted or needed.

That woman, he realized, didn't exist anywhere.

"Heeey, Daniel." A musical male voice spoke from a few feet away. "Long time no see."

Marcus hid his smile as a perky couple approached the booth.

Daniel slid closer to him. "I've been busy." He didn't look up from his drink.

Marcus held back his laughter. It was rare to see the smooth Daniel Ellis squirm but this preppie-swinger-wannabe couple managed it easily.

This time the petite, redheaded female half of the couple spoke. "John and I were hoping to run into you again."

Daniel looked relaxed. Only Marcus noticed the small lines of tension around his blue eyes.

"John, Susan, I told you the last time was really the *last* time." Daniel was being cold and abrupt, entirely unlike his usual suave self.

Amusing as the situation was, he supposed it was time to come to his best friend's aid. It would serve the arrogant bastard right if Marcus got up and left his ass alone.

Sending him a wicked smile, Marcus slid his hand across the table, covering Daniel's fingers with his own. The couple, whom Marcus had privately dubbed "Bondage Barbie and Ken", stared at Marcus for a brief moment before flicking their gazes back to Daniel.

Daniel grabbed the gesture — and Marcus' hand — like the lifeline they were, flipping up his own hand to wrap around Marcus' fingers.

"Besides," Daniel added, finally looking up at the couple. "My schedule is pretty full."

Only Marcus saw the relief in Daniel's sultry smile.

The couple colored, murmured their goodbyes and turned, trying to hide their embarrassment. They left the room without looking back.

Marcus smiled at Daniel's scowl. "What's wrong, Danny-boy? Break another couple's hearts?"

Daniel caught the bartender's attention and signaled for another round. "Broke their hearts? Let me tell you about John and Susan. She's fucking the pool boy, and so is he. Neither of them bothered to inform the other. I found out and disengaged myself from the situation."

Marcus barked out a laugh as Daniel continued. "I don't know who was more broken-hearted, John, Sue or the pool boy. He hit on me too, and I let it slip when I informed them that I wasn't going to see them again. It was a nice two weeks but, damn, it's been over three years now. I am not traveling down that road again."

"Well." Marcus smirked. "You've gotta give them points for being persistent."

Daniel gave him a sour look and reached for his fresh drink. Both sat silent for a moment then Daniel glanced back at his best friend. "Why doesn't it bother you?"

"Why doesn't what bother me?" He returned the glance. He frowned slightly at the uncomfortable expression on Daniel's face.

Daniel's drink arrived, along with the rest of the bottle. The waitress must have figured out this night was going to end at the bottom of that bottle for the two friends. Marcus poured himself another glass.

"Oh, come on, Marcus. Most straight guys would be fucking freaked out being naked in the same room with me." Daniel lowered his voice when heads turned in their direction.

The strong alcohol was spreading its warmth through Marcus' belly. "I don't know, buddy. It might have to do with the fact that we were friends long before I discovered you enjoyed both sides of the fence."

Doubt flashed in Daniel's brilliant blue eyes.

Marcus shrugged. "Hey, with my proclivities I can't very well sit in judgment. Besides, when we share I don't think about that. I think about the woman. Of course, we may have a problem if you ever decide to grab my ass."

His effort to lighten up the subject wasn't working. Daniel looked into the bottom of his glass. "There haven't been as many as people like to think."

Marcus knew that already. While Daniel was attracted to both sexes, he hadn't been with more than a couple of men and those interludes had been brief at best.

"At thirty-six it gets a little old being known for the money you make and the way you fuck." As his mood became darker, Daniel's words began to slur.

They were both a drink away from being really drunk. He gripped Daniel around the back of his neck. "I know man, I know."

The two men sat drinking in complete understanding.

Daniel lifted his glass, and in a rare unguarded moment Marcus saw pain from the past shadowed his face. "Let's make a toast to two of the lousiest fathers ever to grace this earth. And to the most pathetic excuse for a wife and mother who ever was born. Thanks, guys, for turning us into fucking freaks."

"Here, here." Marcus clinked his glass to Daniel's.

Tipping the glass up to his mouth, he halted before the rim touched his lips.

"What the hell?" He closed his eyes, knowing he was seeing things. Opening them again, he let out a rapid string of four-letter words. It was really her. "What the *fuck* is she doing here?"

"Wha'?" Daniel swung his head around in the direction Marcus was looking.

Coming off the dance floor area and into the bar was Marcus' faithful assistant. She looked completely edible, all wide-eyed innocence, flushed from dancing. At least, he thought, dancing had better be all she was flushed from. Dorian Jenner, a longtime friend, the cop who had probably saved his sorry life the night he'd left Karen, and a notorious Dom, had his arm around her waist.

"Woo-hoo!" Daniel hooted drunkenly. "It looks like our little Carrie has a wild streak in her. I knew I really liked her." Daniel's smile widened as he watched Marcus' dark scowl. "Maybe I should go over and say hello."

Marcus slammed his arm across Daniel's chest. "Stay in your seat, Daniel or I'll kick your ass." He scooted up and out of the booth.

Daniel snickered behind him. "Where ya going?"

"To get her the hell away from Jenner and out of here before she gets in over her head," he spat as fury burned in his chest.

Dorian lowered his mouth to Carrie's ear.

"Oh, hell no," Marcus hissed as she gazed laughingly up at the other man.

"Marcus, she's a big girl, man."

He spun around, eyes pinning Daniel to his seat. "What the fuck is that supposed to mean? What's wrong? She's not skinny enough for you?"

Daniel put his hands up. "Whoa, hold on there, buddy. I actually think she's pretty gorgeous, in a good-girl-next-door kind of way."

A muscle jumped in Marcus' clenched jaw.

"I like my girls on the juicy side. You're the scrawny-model-loving man."

Marcus' chest deflated and Daniel drew a breath. "All I meant is that she's old enough to decide where to spend her evenings."

Marcus dragged his fingers through his hair. "How the hell does she even know about this place? Who the hell sponsored her to get in?"

A nonmember couldn't just wander onto the second floor of the club. Those who just came to dance and have a night out didn't own the specially made coins needed to gain access to the private and VIP levels.

And a serious Dom like Jenner wouldn't have danced with just anyone.

He slowly turned back to the table, carefully eyeing his best friend as an appalling idea formed in his alcohol-fogged brain. "Why aren't you surprised to see my assistant on the second floor?"

Daniel shrugged, bringing his drink to his mouth. "I may have sponsored her." Tossing back the scotch, he wasn't prepared when Marcus reached across the table and grabbed his shirt.

"What the hell were you thinking? This is *Carrie* we're talking about."

Daniel carefully removed Marcus' hands from his shirt. "Back off, man. She asked me. I didn't go to her. I questioned her, especially knowing who she is. She knew exactly what she'd find here."

Marcus wasn't convinced, and at the moment it was all he could do to keep from climbing over the table and punching his best friend in the mouth, and then going over and mashing Jenner's mouth, which currently attached to Carrie's knuckles and traveling up her arm.

"She knows what she wants." Daniel's voice lost its hint of mockery. "She knows why she wants it and is exploring her options. Brady accepted her application, so when she asked, I agreed to sponsor her."

Marcus shook his head and walked away before he seriously hurt his best friend. What the hell had the man been thinking? Carrie in this place? She was too…too…innocent. That's what she was, too damn innocent to know what she was doing.

He made his way straight to Carrie and Jenner's table and stopped in front of them.

"Marcus, it's good to see you," the tall, brown-haired Dom acknowledged him.

Marcus' eyes cut to the other man, currently rubbing the palm and playing with the fingers of *his* assistant.

"Excuse us," Marcus said, gently removing her hand from Jenner's and guiding her to her feet.

Jenner let go of her but raised a speculative brow at Marcus as he pulled her toward the door.

"Marcus, what are you doing?" Her startled cry didn't slow his pace at all until they were outside and in the parking lot.

He started walking up and down the aisles of parked cars. His anger was off the charts and he didn't trust himself to slow down and face her.

"Where is it?" he barked, pulling her down another row, trying to find her blue Dodge Intrepid.

"Where is what? What are you doing?" Carrie planted her feet, forcing him to stop or pull her to the ground.

"Where the hell did you park?"

She shook her arm loose. "I came with some friends."

Marcus grunted. Yeah, some friends, bringing her into a meat market like this. It wasn't safe for an untried woman like Carrie.

She may have talked a good game to Daniel, convincing him to sponsor her, but Marcus knew damn good and well she had no real clue what this lifestyle was like. He hauled her out of the parking lot and around to the back of the building.

"Quit manhandling me," she cried.

Marcus froze where he stood. She thought this was rough treatment? He took her upper arms, walking her backward until her back touched the concrete wall. Her brown eyes widened, hopefully out of fear, but he wasn't quite sure.

"Manhandling you?" His voice low, deep and dangerous, he watched as she trembled. "Carrie, where do you think you are exactly?"

She raised her chin a notch. "I know exactly where I am and frankly it's none of your damn business."

"Then you know that this doesn't even come near to the 'manhandling' you'd get from one of the Doms inside."

"Jeez, Marcus. How stupid do you think I am?" She shook her head at him pityingly. "The manhandling I'd get in there would be about ultimately feeling good, and it would be something I agreed to in advance. We're not having sex here. You're trying to intimidate me." She snorted at his glowering expression. "Big difference, boss-man."

Marcus' chest heaved in frustration and shock. His cock hardened when she raised that small chin in defiance. And her sassy mouth was just begging to be silenced by his. At this moment he wanted nothing more than to shove her against the wall and show her what it really meant to be *manhandled*. All of his instincts screamed at him to take her now. The thought shook him to the core. It had been years since he'd had such an animal reaction to soft female skin.

"It's time to go home. You don't belong here." He was getting her the hell out of here. No fucking way was Carrie staying another minute so some asshole could feel her up, or worse take her into one of the VIP suites. Hell, he needed her gone so that it wasn't *him* taking her back to his suite and giving her exactly what she'd come here to discover.

Carrie placed her hands on Marcus' solid chest and pushed hard. He stepped back and straightened, not touching her but still preventing her escape.

He exhaled, obviously trying to calm himself down. Maybe he realized that yelling at her wasn't going to help.

"Carrie, it's natural to be curious after the whole divorce thing and the media coverage, but that was so long ago. What do you hope to gain by coming here now?"

"This isn't about you and your divorce. This is about me."

His gray eyes turned stormy as he took a step forward. She pressed herself into the wall. He was altogether too close.

"Are you sure, Carrie? Are you sure you didn't get just a little bit curious after all the stuff you heard and think it might be fun to experiment?" He inched even closer, his anger still present despite the softening of his voice.

"I know you stumbled on some things in my bathroom at the office. Is that the reason you're here?" His hand traveled down her jaw as he made her face him.

"Tell me, did you fantasize about being tied to my big leather chair while I worked a toy deep inside you?" He traced a lazy path down her chin, past her neck. "I bet I could make you purr, drive you insane for my touch, my cock, my whip."

Carrie's face flamed. Oh shit, this was her boss talking to her like this. The one man whose touch, whose cock, whose whip she'd dreamed of. She should have been furious. If any other man had treated her this way, she would have been. Instead her thighs trembled as the images Marcus described flashed though her mind. She swallowed the moan threatening to break free.

"Marcus, you're a horse's ass, do you know that?" She was pleased her voice came out firm and strong. She was even more pleased when his eyes widened in surprise at her condemnation. He was a harsh man and people rarely ever disrespected him on any level.

"The world does not revolve around you and your penis. I came here because I wanted to. Do you think your need to dominate is any different than my need to…" She cut herself off. Okay, maybe she wasn't as brave as she claimed. She wasn't a complete stranger to this lifestyle. Her last lover, while not a Dom, had been very commanding and had shown her things she never dreamed she would like. She'd fantasized about taking it further, but he never pushed it and soon their time together had fizzled out.

This was her first time in this sort of club. She'd known Marcus came here and shouldn't have been surprised to see him. What did throw her was his total overreaction to her presence. True, they were close as boss and employee. She knew things about his personal life and about him that probably no one else, even his brother or sister, knew. After ten years of working at Worthington, she was a valuable asset. Sadly, she realized that while she knew a lot about Marcus and his family, he knew next to nothing about her.

Marcus never asked, and Carrie never offered any information about her life outside of Worthington. He'd never looked at her as anything other than a trusted assistant who knew her job well and took care of the details.

That disinterest on his part had been one of the factors motivating her little field trip tonight. The realization that he'd never see her as anything but an efficient employee had convinced her that it was time to part company with her sexy, commanding boss.

Carrie knew it was time to get away from him. Whether she wanted to go back into the club or simply call a cab, she wasn't sure, but it was definitely time to go.

Before she was able to turn and run, he had her pinned to the wall, his thigh between hers. Her skirt rode high as he grabbed both wrists roughly and held them over her head.

"Is this what you want?" he whispered in her ear. She shook as fire sizzled down her spine. "You want to be at a man's mercy?" Marcus' breath bathed her face, hot and damp and scented with liquor, his mouth a scant inch from her own. "At *my* mercy?"

His eyes blazed as they bored into hers.

"Do you want to feel my hand on your ass as you're tied tightly to my bed and you're unable to move?" He leaned his body into the cradle of her lower belly.

Her eyes widened as she felt the unmistakable outline of his very rigid cock through his pants.

"Answer me, Carrie. Do you dream of being stretched, toyed with, pushed beyond anything you have ever known to give your master the pleasure he demands?" His finger slid achingly, slowly down the front of her black satin blouse, traveling to her belly, where he made lazy circles above her hips.

She wanted to climb up his body, her boss, the one man she wasn't able to get out of her head, and kiss him senseless. Marcus Worthington was front and center in all of her fantasies. Especially the ones he was describing now. His six-foot-two frame towered over her. He was fit and strong, the hard planes of his body plastered to her much softer ones. His black hair was tousled as though he'd just climbed out of bed, where she was sure he'd been not long ago. A sharp pain hit her in the middle of her chest as she imagined Marcus with another woman.

"Go home, Carrie." He'd obviously taken her silence for denial. Or fear. "You're in over your head here."

"You bastard. You don't get to tell me what to do. I'm not on company time."

The glaze over Marcus' eyes cleared and he jumped back as though he'd been burned. Without uttering another word, he grabbed her by the hand and dragged her to the VIP parking lot. Opening the back of his limo, he unceremoniously pushed Carrie inside. The doors locked behind her, and she couldn't open them. After a moment, the partition glass lowered and an older gentleman looked back at her through the mirror.

"Where to, miss?"

"How about right here?"

"Can't do that. The boss made it clear, I'm to take you home."

Defeated, Carrie crossed her arms and rattled off her address.

Chapter Three

ร๛

Marcus crumpled the neatly typed resignation letter into a tight ball, ready to throw it in the trash. Stopping, he reminded himself that he couldn't destroy the letter, no matter how much he wanted to.

He smoothed out the single sheet as best he could. Carrie, his right hand for the last ten years, was leaving him.

She'd stood by him when his evil ex-wife divorced him, running interference and refusing to let any of the more vocal and judgmental riffraff anywhere near him. Karen had been out of his life as soon as the check he'd written was deposited into her bank account. Carrie, on the other hand, was more deeply entrenched than ever.

It had been easy to make Karen shut her mouth. She'd signed a nondisclosure agreement at their settlement hearing, and Marcus had given her enough money to ensure she would never have to work another day in her selfish life.

For a while it had left a black mark on him and the Worthington group. During that time, Carrie never judged him, never treated him any differently. On occasion, Marcus had even heard her coming to his defense with employees who felt they had the right to comment on his personal life.

He'd never commented on Karen's accusations, some of which were true, most of which were not. The press had a field day though, branding him a pervert and deviant until the next scandal took the front pages. He was grateful for Carrie; she was his rock. He knew he could always count on her.

He'd fucked up Saturday night at the club and she'd made him pay for it every day this week. Now she was leaving the company, and more importantly leaving him behind. His stomach knotted at the mere thought of not seeing her big brown doe eyes every morning. He'd miss the sight of her generous ass twitching away from him in a huff whenever he disagreed with her.

Marcus smiled. He'd always been attracted to her, even before the divorce, but he wasn't a cheat. He also had his own strict code about getting involved with employees. That belief had prevented him from acting on his impulses more than once where Carrie was concerned.

Finding her at Velvet Ice last Saturday had only made his fantasies that much hotter. Every night and a good part of every day since their confrontation at the back of the building, Marcus dreamed of following through on what he'd inadvertently triggered.

The absolute craving to have her, his way.

He ached to show her all the things she claimed she wanted, to make her feel so good, so satisfied. His cock jumped at the memory of her scent, vanilla and musk. Her very own aroma, signaling her arousal. The mere memory of her scent assaulted his senses and demanded that he claim her. He'd do anything to have that scent on his body, on his sheets.

He was crazy. After the number Karen did on him, he had no intention of getting serious ever again. Trust. His had been shattered by a woman who was supposed to have loved him. He'd never be able to give himself completely to another woman, and he was completely okay with that. But he wanted Carrie, and he wanted to be the one to train her. Not someone like Dorian Jenner. Jenner was a good enough guy but not good enough for Carrie.

The knot in his stomach expanded as he realized that she was no longer going to be his employee. Tapping his pen on the desk, he went over the possibilities that little fact might open up to him.

A plan began to take form and he felt nervous excitement for the first time in years. Anticipation crawled along his nerves as his wicked thoughts heated the blood flowing through his body.

She wanted to be a submissive? Then she would be *his* sub. He would train her, starting tonight and for as many nights as they could stand. Marcus knew deep down that any knowledge of submission Carrie had was peripheral at best. He wasn't about to leave her fantasy to another male, one who may not have the same kind of ethics as Marcus did.

First, though, he needed to make sure she was open to the idea. That Carrie fully understood what it meant to be in his bed. There must be no doubt in her mind; her acceptance had to be one hundred percent. He'd been down the road of deception and betrayal with Karen, and he didn't plan on ever going there again.

He and Carrie had a mutual attraction, Marcus was sure of that. Before the night at the club, he'd noticed how she watched him when she thought he wasn't looking. How her nipples would tighten against her silk blouse when she stared at him too long. Her attraction was confirmed Saturday night. With his thigh wedged tight between hers, he'd felt her arousal hot and wet on his leg, her nipples stabbing into his chest, even her breathing had been ragged by the time he'd finished describing the things he could do to her.

He'd been afraid there would be strain between them after his performance and her reaction, and there was. She was always the consummate professional but it was there in her eyes: the uncertainly, the doubt and, he guessed, a little embarrassment to go along with it.

She'd put considerable distance between them all week. He felt it and it bothered him more than it should have. Now he knew why. He passed his hand over her resignation once more.

He wanted Carrie Anderson. He wanted her tied down, wet and panting for him to take her. He wanted her, face flushed, begging him to let her come and screaming his name when he finally did. Marcus didn't know what being with

Carrie would bring, but he wanted her enough to make the leap of faith it required to take her, to train her, to push this thing between them as far as it could go.

Carrie put the call to Meredith Worthington through, relaying the request for her to join her brother in his office in an hour. Meredith, as usual, was cool and professional.

Carrie had a soft spot in her heart for the woman. While she'd never been as forceful as Marcus or as outgoing as Matthew, Meredith possessed her own quiet charm, a warmth she'd showered on the few people allowed to get close to her. Carrie had considered her a friend, as much as an employer could be.

But Meredith had taken Marcus' divorce and the subsequent media circus extremely hard. When the Worthington name was in shambles, Old Stirling unexpectedly dead, the controversy had affected all three siblings. But Meredith had taken it the worst, almost becoming a recluse, only going to work and home. It seemed such a lonely existence. Carrie had tried to comfort her once but Meredith blocked the attempt, telling Carrie she wouldn't talk about family business with her or with anyone.

She'd held fast to that vow, not speaking to her older brother for almost two months, depending on Carrie to take messages back and forth. It had been a nightmarish time, and finally she told Meredith that she could no longer run interference between the siblings. Meredith apologized in that new, distant way of hers and began delivering her messages herself, but the relationship between brother and sister remained strained.

Carrie hit the intercom and told Marcus that his sister had confirmed their meeting. She swallowed hard as he asked her to come into his office. He'd read the letter she left on his desk earlier that morning. Two more weeks and she would no longer work here.

Carrie didn't want to leave her position but she'd discovered she couldn't work for Marcus anymore, not without her heart being broken. She loved this man more than anything, and watching him waste himself on an endless string of plastic beauty-queen wannabes was slowly sucking the life out of her.

She was no longer willing to make his dinner dates or send morning-after flowers. She couldn't deal with fielding all the calls from the many women he dated. He changed them on a weekly basis but they were all the same. High society, rich and blonde. Willowy debutantes who wanted nothing more than to snatch a millionaire.

Oh, they knew how he liked sex. After the fact that he was a Dom was splashed across the tabloids, there wasn't a person in the social or business circles of the city who didn't know about it. The endless parade of women wanted to change him, make him happy having vanilla sex. Carrie wasn't about to stick around and watch it continue. She couldn't. Not after having a taste of that dark thrill herself. Not when she could still close her eyes and feel him pressed up against her, his cock throbbing against her as he breathed wicked words of desire and submission against her lips.

Taking a deep breath, she braced herself and stepped into her boss's office.

Chapter Four

✄

Marcus looked up from his desk, his dark-gray eyes penetrating right through her, making her hot and needy.

"Want to explain this?" he asked, his face impassive as he waited for her to answer.

Carrie nervously licked her lips, and she thought she saw his eyes widen a bit. No, must have been wishful thinking on her part. Her body was still reeling from the mere memory of how he felt pressed against her.

"I've been offered a better position elsewhere. It pays quite a bit more, and I happen to like the company very much. It's a good move for me." She was relieved to hear the false steadiness in her voice.

"I'll match any offer you've received." He casually leaned back in his chair.

Carrie felt her face burn as thoughts about being tied to that same chair floated through her mind. *God, I'm going crazy,* she thought as her panties dampened.

She shook her head. She wouldn't give in, even though every cell in her body screamed to. "No. I'm sure it's no longer wise for me to work here."

"Why not? Is someone giving you a problem?" His voice had dropped a few octaves, his eyes boring into her.

No one, she mused, *unless you count yourself.*

"I think we both know why I'm no longer comfortable being here." Carrie wouldn't play games. She stood before him, calm on the surface while she tried not to remember the feel of his breath on her face, in her ear. Her "battery operated boyfriend's" motor burning out last night had been the last

36

straw. She couldn't, wouldn't, continue to put herself through this.

Marcus rose from his seat and walked around the desk and up behind her. He placed strong hands on her shoulders, rubbing gently. Her nipples tightened painfully within her silk bra.

"Carrie, you have no reason to be embarrassed. I still don't think you have any business going to that club. I don't want you to go but I don't hold it against you." His deep, smoky voice tickled her ear.

She bristled and eased away from him. Her thighs were moist from his firm touch and she was pissed at herself for having no control. She was even more pissed off at him for being an arrogant, oblivious *man*.

"Please, let's just leave this alone." She faced him. "I gave you my two weeks' notice so that I can train another assistant, and then I'm on my way. There is no changing my mind."

Marcus moved around to the front of his desk and leaned back, crossing his ankles and folding his arms over his chest. "It isn't as easy as you training a replacement. You're under contract to me for another year and three months."

She gasped. "You're going to hold me to that?" She could literally feel her freedom, her escape, slipping away. Tears sprang to the corners of her eyes but she swallowed hard, refusing to cry. That damn contract. She'd forgotten all about signing the thing last year.

His face took on a smug look. "Yes, I think that I am."

She wanted to stomp her foot in anger. Arrogant bastard! After all she'd done for him, working her ass off to help build his business, standing by him when no one else did. Her loyalty to him was unwavering and she had proven it over and over on a daily basis. And this was how he rewarded her?

"You cannot possibly be this selfish, Marcus. I deserve better than this from you." Her voice quivered as her chest began to pound.

He lowered his arms. His handsome face softened a little as he left the desk and stood before her.

"I *can* be this selfish, Carrie. Have you forgotten what a sick, selfish pervert I really am?"

She shook with indignation. "Oh, for crying out loud. That was over years ago, and you know darn good and well that I never thought you were sick or selfish or a pervert." Her face heated like it always did when she came to his defense.

Her reward was his hand cupping the side of her face, the pad of his thumb gliding across her bottom lip. "There's my girl, always coming to my defense."

His face lit up with his dazzling smile. It always amazed Carrie how transformed Marcus was when he smiled. It was a rare sight and she basked in it.

"I have a compromise for you."

It was difficult for her to concentrate with his thumb on her mouth. "Ah... Ok. What is it?" she finally forced out. Better to keep her questions short or he would know for sure how affected she was by his touch.

The musk of his skin washed over her senses, heady and totally masculine. Her mouth watered and she wanted to reach out and lick the pulse point in his neck.

"You spend the weekend with me and I'll let you out of your contract."

She stepped back to get a good look at his face. He was stone-cold serious. Her spine stiffened ramrod straight and a lump formed in her throat, threatening to cut off her air. She had the sudden urge to not only kiss him, but also slap him right across his superior smile. The need to do both weighed heavily upon her. She wasn't a violent woman though, and jumping him was something one of the bimbos he dated would do.

She wanted this. His offer was the culmination of her wildest fantasies, so why pretend to be offended by it? The idea of being with Marcus Worthington started an undeniable ache between her thighs to match the one in her heart.

Marcus watched the wide range of emotions pass across Carrie's lovely, flushed face. Anger and embarrassment gave way to curiosity and then stark need. His dick ached as he waited for her answer. He was patient and let her take as long as she needed. He wondered if her ass would flush that same color of pink after he had given her a special punishment.

She nodded her head briefly, clearly unable to get the word *yes* out. It wasn't good enough for him. She needed to speak her desire for him to master her. Then, and only then, could they begin.

"Carrie, you have to tell me yes. You think you know what a weekend with me will entail. You think you know what I like. On some things you may be right. But I can guarantee there are things you will experience that you never dreamed possible." He approached her again, his hands rising to her shoulders. He let his fingers trail down her chest and brush over her breasts.

She closed her eyes and swallowed a moan.

"The tabloids didn't know half of what I like, so you have to be sure. There's no going back once you walk into my house."

Marcus didn't know if she truly understood what it meant to be a sub or if she could do it. At work she was efficient, sharp and smart. She was capable of holding her own in a male-dominated work environment. Handing over complete control to him might be more than she could handle. A lot of women fantasized about being dominated but far fewer enjoyed the reality of the complex relationship between Dom and sub. Marcus wasn't brutal, nor did he humiliate his lovers. He found those practices distasteful. He did, however, command absolute control during sex. From positions to clothing, even up to and including orgasm, he expected compliance. Unless the safe word was spoken, he did as he pleased.

Carrie's brown eyes were wide. He hadn't meant to scare her. He just wanted her to be sure, because her life was about to change. If they explored this thing between them, by Sunday night she would never be the same woman again.

She drew a deep breath, and when she answered him her words were like music to his ears. "Yes, Marcus, I understand what you're saying and what spending the weekend with you means."

He stepped back and moved to the door, locking it. Returning to stand a few feet in front of her, he rapped out a command. "Unbutton your blouse." He might as well test her now.

When she hesitated, he sighed. "If you're unable to follow a simple command, this isn't going to work."

She took another deep breath and lifted her fingers to the top button of her shirt. Every pearly button she opened revealed more soft, creamy flesh for Marcus' eyes to devour. She let the shirt fall to the floor, trying to suck in her belly.

"Don't present yourself to me any other way than how you really are." He kept his voice purposely severe. "There is no shame in showing your body to the one who owns it when he tells you to."

Her tits were pushed into a white satin bra, cleavage spilling out the tops. He clenched his hands, making fists at his sides. He wanted to feel her so badly but he was going to make them both wait.

"Unhook the bra."

This time she complied with no hesitation. Reaching back, she snapped the hook. The straps fell down her arms and she pulled the bra off in an inadvertent striptease. It landed on top of her blouse. As her full breasts spilled from confinement, he noticed her rosy nipples were puckered and begging for his teeth. *Not yet, not yet*, became his mantra.

"Touch your nipples."

She gently grasped her breasts. Her eyes were cast downward, refusing to meet his. He would have to work on that. He liked a woman to look at him whenever he was doing something to her or when she was pleasing herself at his request. There was nothing sexier than a pair of half-hooded eyes shining with delight.

Marcus rubbed the front of his pants, no longer bothering to hide his erection. His hand settled on the line parallel with his zipper. The motion seemed to set her off because she started to pluck at her stiff nipples, rolling them between her thumb and finger.

"Pull up your skirt." Marcus found it hard to keep his voice even and had to throttle back a moan as her skirt traveled up, showing even more of that creamy, smooth skin.

"Lose the pantyhose." He wanted her in stockings or nothing at all.

She slid her small hands down her thighs, kicking off her shoes. Her tits swung with the motion as she pushed her hose completely off. This time a moan did escape as Marcus imagined grabbing those rounded globes and palming them hard while he ground his erection into that generous ass and his mouth was locked on the nape of her neck, marking her as his.

Carrie straightened and lifted her skirt to the top of her soft thighs. White satin panties failed to hide the dark patch between her legs. Damn, she was juicy.

Her body was pale and soft. The total opposite of the women he usually bedded. His body came alive as he imagined sinking into her pliant flesh. *Fuck* was the only coherent thought running through his traitorous mind.

"Take off the panties then turn around and place your hands on the wall." His voice was much harsher this time. He was trying to get some control over himself; anything to keep from slamming into her now. Marcus wanted to draw this out, to make it last. Wanted her so needy that she'd do anything he asked.

The idea of her bound to his bed, her heart-shaped ass in the air while he took her, taunted him, made him crazy. He hadn't felt desire this intense in years. Long before his marriage. Hell, maybe all the way back to when he was a fucking eighteen-year-old kid discovering the pleasures of dominating a woman for the first time.

He stalked over to her, leaning into her and letting her feel his heat. He knew she felt his hard dick pressing into her ass. He brushed his hands along the insides of her legs, starting at her knees and working his way steadily up.

"Press your ass out, Carrie, and spread your legs wide. I want to see all of you," he murmured, an unfamiliar hunger making his voice gravelly.

She pushed that fantastically full ass out and spread her thighs wide open for his view. His hand went between her legs, moving along her pussy lips. They were bare and so fucking silky to the touch. His mouth watered with the desire to take those sweet lips into his mouth.

Running his middle finger down her moist slit and up to her ass, he circled the petal opening and whispered, "Have you ever been taken here?" He pressed his finger lightly against the barrier, and she gasped.

When she shook her head no, Marcus continued, "Have you ever had anything in your ass, Carrie?"

Her head hit the wall. "Yes, a plug."

"How often?" He pressed his face to her cheek, his mouth less than an inch from her mouth. "Answer me, Carrie. How often do you push a plug up this delicious ass of yours?"

"A few...a few times a week," she whispered. Marcus gathered more of her moisture on his finger and slid it back between her cheeks, sliding the tip into her. He wiggled it slightly back and forth. She relaxed immediately and he knew she would take his cock tonight, anywhere he wanted to give it to her.

"When you fuck yourself? Is that when you use it? Or do you let your lover give you that pleasure?"

He didn't want to think why the answer was so important to him, but it was. The idea of another man touching her this way brought a swift ribbon of anger swelling through him, demanding that he take her and make her forget about any other man she ever let touch her body.

"There's no one. I use it on myself," she cried as he swirled his finger around once more before pulling out.

With one hand, he opened her swollen lower lips, spreading them wide. The other slipped around her drenched hole and up to her clit. It wasn't large but it was so hard. He pinched it lightly between his fingers, drawing a whimper from her. It wouldn't take much for her to come quickly but Marcus wouldn't allow that.

"You can't come, ever, unless I say you can. Otherwise I'll be forced to punish you."

He didn't think she was listening. Instead she was rubbing herself against his hand. He abruptly stopped his stroking, placing a smack on her left ass cheek before continuing to play with her clit. He thrust his finger into her and slapped her other cheek, harder this time. She moaned but stilled her movements. Her ass did indeed turn a delicious shade of pink, and Marcus forced himself not to go to his knees and taste her then and there.

He removed his hand and turned her around. Her light brown hair was plastered against her face, her breathing was shallow. She was trembling with the need to orgasm, and Marcus knew that it was the most beautiful thing he had ever seen.

"On your knees, Carrie," he ordered.

Chapter Five

ည

Carrie knelt on shaky knees. She felt like she was going to float away on her unfulfilled pleasure. Hands at her sides, she waited for his next move. Reading up on submission and playing a little bit with her last boyfriend hadn't prepared her for the feelings flying in her bloodstream now.

Experiencing this with Marcus was a totally different animal than what she had with Charles, her old boyfriend. Her emotions were bouncing all over the place. Excitement, desire, wanting to please, they were all playing havoc with her mind. She loved the idea of her choices being guided by another. It was heaven not to have to think about what to do, only to obey and feel.

"Spread your knees," he rapped out, eyeing her critically. She quickly complied, spreading her knees wide, ready for his touch. "Now lift your breasts." He contemplated the soft, white flesh with obvious greed. "They are mine, and you will always offer them to me."

With every command, she watched his cock swell more. With every command, she felt the moisture slide down the inside of her thighs. She was afraid that if he said much more, permission or not, she would come like she'd never come before.

"Shoulders back. And look at me. This is your presentation position." Rubbing one big hand along the length of his cock, he walked slowly around her, examining her posture. "This is the position you will always take with me until I give you other instructions." He came around to face her again and reached out, tapping her full lower lip with one hard finger. "Do you understand?"

Carrie nodded mutely. She wanted nothing more than to offer herself to this man.

He slid the zipper of his Armani pants down, and the sound echoed in her ears. He let them drop and they pooled around his ankles. His thighs were thick and muscled, sprinkled with a light dusting of dark hair. Next came his black boxer briefs, which he tugged down without ceremony, letting his long, thick cock spring free.

Carrie stared in wonder as his dick descended toward her mouth, a liquid bead suspended on the wide head. The shaft was lined with a thick vein running underneath. His balls were heavy and tightened before her very eyes.

He grabbed her hair, sliding his fingers though the sides, securing the silky strands with both hands.

"I want you to suck my cock. Do not come. Do you understand, woman?"

A shiver of delight passed through her at the way he said *woman*, so possessive, so dark.

She smiled at him and he seemed to take that as a yes. His cocked bumped her bottom lip. She snaked her tongue out to greedily lap at the silky drop on the thick head. He tasted salty, slightly bitter, his scent heady. Carrie moved her head forward; she wanted to feel his length in her mouth. She was stopped short by a tug on her hair.

"You will drink every drop. Do you understand? I want to feel all of it sliding down that beautiful throat."

She answered with a small nod and that seemed to be enough for Marcus. She ran her tongue all around the head before sliding it along the side of his shaft. He was so hard yet velvety soft at the same time. Carrie adored the feel of him on her tongue.

His eyes slid closed as she finally took him fully into her mouth, opening as wide as possible to accommodate his girth. Slowly, savoring his taste, she sucked him in and out, taking his cock a little bit farther with each shallow thrust.

She cupped his heavy sac, massaging him lightly, and fondled his tight balls in her palm.

"Yeah, that's it. Take me all the way in," Marcus ground out between clenched teeth. Carrie's mouth was so fucking hot on his cock, licking and sucking him as if her life depended on it. A lot of women hated doing this. Not his Carrie. She was reveling in it. She moaned against his sensitive skin, sending flames along his spine.

Her mouth was made to suck him. He pushed in a little quicker, tightening his hold on her hair. She rounded her mouth even more for him, relaxing her throat so that he felt it with the tip of his dick.

Marcus opened his eyes, looking down at her, watching her through slit lids. "Touch yourself, Carrie, but don't come."

Her hand tentatively slipped between her thighs. The tips of her fingers brushed lightly over her clit.

"Faster, Carrie, harder. Show me how you get off." He hoped that she *would* come so that he had a reason to punish her sweet ass. "Slide two fingers inside your cunt."

She never took her mouth from his cock as she thrust two fingers into herself. Her moan vibrated through his length. The feeling resonated throughout his legs, right down to his toes.

He gazed, fascinated, as she continued to play with herself. Everything about her was begging to be spanked, and he couldn't wait to oblige her. He'd always known she'd be hot. What he hadn't counted on was how well he fit in her mouth. He was dying to get inside the rest of her.

Carrie's head bobbed in perfect sync with his thrusts. Her hand playing with his balls was surprisingly rough and he loved every fucking second of it.

The pressure built in his back as his balls tightened against his flesh. Marcus held her head still as he pumped into her warm, wet mouth.

The sight of his cock sliding between her plump lips as she churned her fingers in her cunt sent him over the edge. He drove his dick into her once, twice, three times before shooting his come deep into her mouth, roaring his pleasure for the world to hear.

She continued to swallow as he kept releasing himself into her throat. Her body stiffened and a cry escaped, announcing her own orgasm.

He let go of her hair once he'd caught his breath.

"I told you not to come." His voice was stern and she blushed.

"I'm sorry…I'm sor…"

Marcus shushed her with a finger to her lips. "I will have to punish you tonight, Carrie. Do you understand?"

She gave a small nod. She looked nervous but not afraid. More eager than anything.

He tucked himself back into his pants and helped Carrie to her feet. He bent and retrieved her shirt and bra. He held her bra out, noting the size as she put her arms through the straps. He stepped behind her and hooked it. He slid the blouse up as she eased her arms into it. Going back to the front of her, Marcus buttoned every one of the damned pearly buttons, cursing when he had to start over because he'd pushed a button through the wrong hole. He helped her straighten her skirt.

She picked up her hose but Marcus shook his head, holding out his hand. Carrie placed the nylons across his palm. She watched, silent and wide-eyed as he balled them up and threw them in the trash.

He went to his desk, taking a moment to write down a list of instructions. He gave the slip of paper to her; she took it, glancing down, her forehead scrunching up.

"Your attire will be waiting for you at that store. I want you to pick it up by three o'clock. You're to go home and dress exactly in the first outfit. Then you're to drive to my home by no later than five."

He unlocked the door then returned to her side and wrapped his hands around her shoulders. He'd opened his mouth to tell her that she'd done well, but before he could utter a word his office door opened and Meredith strode in.

"Carrie said you needed to see me." Meredith's clipped voice seemed to break the magic spell that had taken control of the room. Marcus' sister froze then looked from him to Carrie. Her eyes narrowed and Marcus knew there was no mistaking that something had gone on in this room before Meredith had arrived.

Carrie's normally polished appearance was gone. In its place was the image of a goddess — her face pink, lips bruised and plump, legs slightly wobbly. When she attempted to walk out the door, she was looking at him rather than where she was going and practically walked right into the frame.

Her face flushed scarlet as she muttered, "Oops!"

Marcus couldn't contain his chuckle as she righted herself and rushed out. This weekend was going to push his ability to remain in control. He relished a challenge, and his curvy little *ex-assistant* was going to prove one hell of a challenge.

"Have you lost your mind?" Meredith bit out. "You must have lost your mind. Tell me this is a joke. It's not enough that you're the most notorious Dom in the greater Detroit area, but now you're banging your secretary? Jesus, Marcus." She cast a regretful glance after Carrie's retreating figure. "You're going to ruin her."

Marcus gave a weary sigh. "Carrie is no longer an employee at The Worthington Group. Now, I need you to take the six o'clock meeting I had scheduled with Renatto Construction. I'm leaving in an hour and will be unreachable this weekend."

Meredith pointed her finger at him, and Marcus braced himself for her meltdown.

Her silver eyes narrowed. "You listen here, big brother. If you think I am going to go through another scandal like the one you and Karen brought down on this family, you are mistaken."

He allowed her this momentary rant. He always did. No one talked to him about his personal life like Meri. No one else would dare. He just couldn't bring himself to tell her to piss off. The memories of sitting at their father's funeral were forever burned into his mind. Not of the "Old Man" lying in the casket, but of his baby sister.

Meredith had borne the brunt of their father's disappointment in every situation, from bad business deals to his eldest son's failures. Marcus, wrapped up in his own world, had failed to protect her from Stirling, and that had never been more apparent than at the funeral. The sick feeling returned as he remembered her sitting, cold and silent, the vivid bruise on her cheek a throbbing reminder of how he'd failed her.

Her eyes sliced through him. He'd betrayed her in more ways than one that last week. Treated her no better than their father. Had even treated her worse, because she'd trusted him in ways she'd never trusted the Old Man. That betrayal had changed Meri forever, and not in a good way. It had changed Marcus as well, pulled him back from the tight line he was walking. He'd almost crossed that line, almost proved he was no better than Stirling.

His father's death and Meri's self-imposed exile from the world showed Marcus just how close he'd come to losing his soul.

So Marcus allowed her the leeway he'd never give another individual. It was the only way he knew to try to make up for the life she'd led before their father died.

And for the things he'd said to her that last, furious night. He desperately longed to see her laugh and smile, to relax and have fun. She had an old soul, and Marcus wanted nothing more than to hold her and tell her he was sorry for being the biggest asshole to walk the planet. But he knew Meri would never allow that. Just as she never allowed anyone to touch her for more than a moment before withdrawing.

He patiently waited for her to wind down. When the proverbial shit had hit the fan and the world found out he enjoyed a whip and rope instead of wine and roses, he had just given Meredith every reason to believe he had no respect for his lovers. Remembering his harsh words in the face of her own budding sensuality, he understood her reaction. But in the end, he couldn't give up this chance to be with Carrie, even for the sister he loved and had betrayed.

"Play your little games on your own time, Marcus." The finality in her voice was nothing new. It had been there for the last five years.

He walked over to her, putting a reassuring arm around her stiff form. As he walked her to the door, he plucked her nose. It was a gesture of affection, and a thing Marcus did that made her crazy and ready to spit nails.

"Meredith, you worry too much."

"Marcus, you don't worry enough."

"I'm sorry, sis. Like I said, Carrie no longer works here. You have nothing to worry about."

She started to walk out when Marcus' grip stopped her.

"One of these days, Meredith, a man will bring you to your knees. Then what will you do?"

"Oh, Marcus. In order for that to happen I'd have to have a heart." She turned her back on him and stalked from the office.

* * * * *

An hour later, Marcus watched hungrily as Carrie left the office to prepare for their weekend. He was anticipating this forbidden little liaison more than he'd anticipated anything for years. Picking up his phone, he dialed. It was answered on the third ring.

"I need you tonight."

Daniel's silky smooth voice vibrated with laughter. "Already? I thought you'd be out of commission for a while…" He just laughed harder at Marcus' low growl. "Do you need me to call ahead and have the room prepared?"

"No, we're not going to the club. Be at my house by nine. Use your key. I'll be busy."

Surprise came clearly from the other end of the line. "Your house? We've never, not at the house."

Why did Daniel have to be so fucking obvious? "I know. Now, are you coming or not?" He was not up for explanations, though he couldn't have said why.

"Yeah, I'll be there, man," Daniel replied slowly.

Marcus didn't like the speculation in his friend's voice. Not one little bit.

"Fine," he rapped out in full Dom mode. Then, picturing Carrie's wide eyes, he added, "And Daniel, this is a novice we'll be dealing with."

"Oh, so this is serious, sharing with a newbie. Do I know the lucky lady?" Daniel was getting way too much enjoyment from this conversation.

Marcus wasn't sure whether to keep it secret until tonight or to go ahead and confess. He decided on the latter. "Yeah, you do. It's Carrie."

"Have you lost your fucking mind?" Daniel's silky smooth voice went razor sharp. "I thought you weren't going there."

"So did I, but when she tried to quit today…"

"She tried to quit?" Daniel cut him off. "What the hell did you do to her?"

Marc pinched the bridge of his nose. "I fucked up when I dragged her out of the club Saturday and it's been hell all week because of it. She says she has another job."

Daniel snorted. "Then tell me, how did she end up going from quitting to spending the night with you?"

"She's under contract and I politely reminded her of that little fact. I said the only way I would accept her resignation was if she spent the weekend with me so that I could teach her how to be a submissive."

Laughter rang on the other end of the phone. "The great Marcus Worthington resorting to blackmail? Damn! It seems sweet little Carrie lit some kind of fire under you Saturday."

"So it would appear," Marcus mumbled. It was true. Somehow his efficient assistant had gotten one up on him. Well, tonight he would repay the favor.

"I suppose I could offer her a position in my new Ann Arbor office."

A vicious pit opened up in Marcus' stomach. "Oh, hell no."

Marcus was sure half the outer office heard him holler. Carrie? Working for Daniel? No way in hell was that going to happen. Daniel didn't have a no-sleeping-with-your-employees rule in *his* office. "I should kick your ass for even suggesting it, my friend."

Daniel only grunted at his threat. "Why do you keep getting pissed at me? You're letting her go, right?"

Marcus didn't even dignify Daniel's lame justification with an answer. He didn't want her to leave the company, or him for that matter, but she wanted to go. He'd have to be satisfied with the weekend.

"Marcus." Daniel's voice regained some of its usual velvet. "Haven't you figured it out yet?"

"Figured out that you want to fuck her, you mean?" His teeth clenched so hard the words barely made it through the phone.

"Man, you're blind. You want her. You've *always* wanted her. I think she got tired of the parade of chicks you go through on a monthly basis. I never planned on seducing her."

"Yeah, right. And how do I know you aren't lying through those perfectly capped teeth, Daniel?"

"My teeth are not capped, thank you very much. I'm naturally gorgeous." Marcus snorted but Daniel ignored him and continued. "I don't plan to seduce her, because *you* want her. I haven't forgotten your reaction at the club. Have you?"

"Of course I haven't. And don't be ridiculous. My reaction was because Carrie was too innocent to be there, especially with Dorian Jenner sniffing around."

Daniel laughed, one of his controlled *you really amuse me* kind of laughs.

"Cut the shit, Marcus. This has been brewing for as long as she's worked there. You get a look in your eye whenever you're around her. Hell, you didn't even look at Karen like that and she was your fucking wife."

He didn't acknowledge Daniel's unwanted observations. If he did, he'd have to consider that he wanted more from Carrie than a weekend of hot sex. And if he considered that, he couldn't be with her at all. Not when he couldn't allow it to lead to more.

He refused to even consider anything that might keep him from taking what he wanted from her tonight, but he did consider excluding Daniel from his plans. On some deep, visceral level, he really didn't want to share her. And the idea of Daniel of all people touching all that silky white skin made him almost crazy. It was that realization that made him certain he had to stick with the plan.

No, he wasn't changing his plans. He needed this, and maybe Carrie did as well. More than that, he needed Daniel to be there, although his deviously sneaky ass didn't deserve it.

"After tonight, don't even think about offering her a job."

"Too late."

Now Marcus knew Daniel had lost his fucking mind.

"You're the new job she has waiting for her?" His voice exploded.

"Don't try and pull your Dom routine on me, pal, it won't work. I don't like being tied up and bossed around."

Marcus snorted in disgust.

Daniel continued in a more serious voice, "I won't have her work directly for me. She's a damn good assistant. I may be your best friend but I'm not a fool. She's a good woman, and I'm not going to refuse to help her just to satisfy your inner caveman."

"Just be at the house!" Slamming down the phone, Marcus stood up and began pacing his office.

Chapter Six

✂

The drive to Marcus' house was excruciating. Even the beautiful view through the car window failed to calm Carrie's nerves. Her body was still in overdrive from their encounter at the office. As she'd prepared herself for him, she'd brought herself to orgasm in the shower out of sheer desperation. It still wasn't enough. Driving down Telegraph Road, she felt every bump and groove in the asphalt. Tonight she would feel Marcus inside of her.

Five years of fantasy were about to come to life.

For the first five years she'd worked for him, Carrie had only thought of her boss in a professional manner. True, he was gorgeous in a rough sort of way. Not Hollywood handsome like his best friend Daniel, but very compelling, very commanding. During his messy divorce, when the city found out how Marcus enjoyed sex, a light bulb turned on in Carrie's head. The bits and pieces of his sex life that were revealed had excited her almost unbearably. That's when she had begun to look at her boss in a different light.

She'd begun to look at herself in a different light too. Carrie was determined to be a good submissive. She'd always felt a need deep in her soul, she just hadn't been able to put a name to it. It was only after Marcus' scandal that she realized there was a name for the feelings she was experiencing: sexual submission. This led her to exploring the world of Doms and subs through books and her computer. The word "Dominant", she'd learned, was a blanket description for many levels of fetish play. Some people only wanted to be tied, some whipped hard.

Carrie knew that she could never delve into the darker side of BDSM. She couldn't imagine he was into that kind of pain but if Marcus pushed her in a direction she didn't want to go, she'd be out of there fast.

She'd gone out on a few dates with one self-proclaimed Dom but the chemistry just wasn't there. He wanted a twenty-four-hour-a-day slave. Carrie didn't fit into that category. She'd happily submit in the bedroom, but outside in the real world she expected to be treated as an equal. The way Marcus always treated her.

Marcus. It all came back to him, every fantasy and every desire. The truth was, Carrie could only picture herself submitting to him, and no other.

She flipped the air conditioner on as her body temperature climbed. Catching herself in the rearview mirror, she still couldn't believe Marcus had actually blackmailed her into this weekend.

Gazing out the windshield, she enjoyed the view. It was a busy time of day, with men and women driving home to start their weekends. She wondered who among them felt the way she did. Which ones had lovers waiting at home for them to come through the door?

His house was incredible, Carrie thought, looking up at the two-story colonial. While it wasn't as big as others in the neighborhood, it was stunning nonetheless. The red brick set off the black shutters and ornate wooden door. The landscaping was professionally done and called to mind an old-fashioned, formal garden.

She climbed the three stone steps to his door and gathered her nerve. She reached up to knock, and the door swung open before she even touched the wood.

Marcus greeted her with a smile; she rocked back a little on her feet. He was gorgeous, dressed casually in a pair of faded denim jeans that molded his thighs to perfection. The sleeves of his white button-down shirt were rolled up to his elbows, revealing finely honed arms. The top three buttons were open, showing a light dusting of back hair she knew would trail down his belly and into those jeans.

She flushed as her lower body moistened. The butterflies in her stomach turned into battering rams. The back of her neck heated up and her nipples tightened painfully as she gazed at his full mouth.

Holding the door open, he reached out to take her hand, enfolding it in his larger one and squeezing ever so lightly. Carrie's steps were unsure and stilted as she entered the marble-floored foyer.

Seeming to sense her trepidation, Marcus turned to her. He shut the door with a thud and slowly backed her against it. He stroked across her jawline as he looked at her. His gray eyes took on a smoky quality. She wasn't able to hold his penetrating gaze and flicked her eyes downward. She swallowed hard at the lump forming in her throat.

"If you're not sure about this, I'll let you leave now with no hard feelings." Concern etched the hard planes of his face. "I won't hold you to our bargain."

He was giving her an out. Carrie's heart squeezed. She wanted, more than anything, to believe that this meant he cared for her as more than an employee. As more than just a friend. In truth, she knew it just meant that he was a decent man. A cautious man who wouldn't open himself up to possible accusations later. No, she wasn't backing out of fulfilling her dream.

She lowered her eyes and tried to toughen her heart. "No, I don't want out of this."

He tipped her chin up with one finger, forcing her to meet his eyes.

Trapped in their smoky depths, she decided to let her feelings show. "I've wanted to be with you this way for a long time now."

She heard a low sigh slide from him as his hand slid under her chin. Pressing his body flush with hers, he took her mouth. No soft beginning, this kiss was a full-on assault. He tasted like peppermint candy as he rubbed his tongue along her lips. Carrie grabbed the front of his shirt, bunching it in her fists.

The door and his body were the only things holding her up. She was weakening from his kisses, swooning. She'd read about women swooning from passion and thought it a joke. How did a woman become so overwhelmed by a kiss? She understood now.

Marcus' mouth kept coming back for more, tasting, teasing, his tongue slipping in and out. She tried to pull him even closer but he broke their kiss.

He slid his hands down each of her arms, grasping each wrist. Wrapping his hands around them firmly, he raised them above her head.

"You're not allowed to touch me until I tell you how and where." He leaned in, biting the side of her jaw. "Do you understand me, Carrie?" His voice was filled with deep, dark promises.

Carrie could only nod her assent. He slanted his head slightly. Putting both of her wrists in one of his hands, he touched her cheek, opening her mouth wider. When she was positioned to his liking, he took her again, devouring her. He forcefully pushed her knees apart. The loose, thin material of her skirt rose. Marcus ground his knee against the apex of her thighs, startling a breathy cry from her.

His mouth left hers, traveling down her cheek, licking the sensitive skin behind her ear. She turned her head to give him better access and he groaned his appreciation. He coaxed her tongue into his mouth. When she complied, he ground his knee a little harder, hitting her clit. She moaned into his mouth and he sucked it into him. Bringing his hand up to her hair, he slid his fingers in, tightening his hold. He tilted her head to the left, his mouth biting a trail across the soft flesh at her neck.

The nips and bites were eased by his tongue afterward. Her pussy was drenched and aching; she was ready to come against his hard thigh.

He let go of her arms, leaning back enough to place his hand over the front of her throat. His eyes were more silver now than gray as they took her in.

"Rule. Number. One." He emphasized each word with his knee, moving it back and forth against her weeping flesh. "You can never come until I say you can. If you come before I tell you to, I will punish you. In fact—" His eyes filled with evil anticipation. "I already owe you for this afternoon at the office."

She closed her eyes, goose bumps rising on her skin. The idea of him delivering a punishment gave her chills as she imagined the pleasure he could deliver. Carrie wanted everything he had to offer. She had two days to store up enough memories of belonging to Marcus Worthington to last a lifetime.

"It's time to begin."

* * * * *

This wasn't exactly how she'd pictured the start of their evening. Marcus said nothing as he drove to the small Italian restaurant. Carrie smiled at the maître d' as he seated them in a dimly lit back corner. It was a perfect place for lovers to meet. Their cozy table for two was lit with only one candle, and the light cast shadows across Marcus' handsome face.

Menus were placed in front of them. Nervously, Carrie opened hers, perusing what they had to offer. Marcus scooted next to her so that his thigh touched hers.

"I hope you're not thinking about ordering a salad for dinner." His palm slid along the top of her silk-covered knee, raising the skirt of her dress a bit higher. He found the lace at the top of her thigh-high stockings and squeezed.

She jumped from the electrical current shooting through her. She'd never worn anything but pantyhose before. The silk stockings felt decadent against her skin, as did the high-cut lace panties and matching bra he'd instructed her to wear.

At first Carrie had balked at the idea that Marcus had gotten her size correct when she picked up the clothes. There was something so embarrassing that he'd be so intimately aware her size was in the double digits. She got over it, though, when she remembered the look on his face as he took in her bare breasts. He didn't mind her extra padding, and under his gaze she truly felt sexy for the first time in her life.

Marcus traced lazy circles around the exposed flesh at the top of her thighs. The teasing touch made Carrie fidgety. Oh, why the hell had he brought her to dinner? She'd much rather be in his bed.

He leaned in close and bit her earlobe. "Stop wiggling around. I want to enjoy the touch of your skin."

The waitress came over and asked if they were ready to order. When Carrie couldn't find her voice, Marcus chuckled.

"Shall I?" he asked.

She nodded and allowed him to order for her. She wasn't certain what he said to the waitress. All she knew for sure was that his fingers were sliding farther and farther up her thigh and touching her lace-covered pussy.

Wine was poured for each of them. Carrie reached for her glass but Marcus beat her to it. He tasted her wine, sliding his tongue discreetly along the rim, and then brought the glass to her lips. He tilted the rich red liquid into her mouth and she swallowed. No man had ever done that before and she was shaken by the intimacy.

"Open your thighs, Carrie." Marcus' voice had that low, in-command tone that drove her wild. She stared, eyes wide. He didn't actually mean to do something *here*, did he? They were in public for Pete's sake.

"Open now, Carrie."

She slowly spread her legs. He pushed her panties to the side, exposing slick, wet skin. The tip of his finger slid up and down her slit. She couldn't stop her knees from moving inward as if to capture his finger.

"Open, Carrie." He continued to sip his wine while creating havoc between her thighs. She was thankful for the dark atmosphere in the restaurant, otherwise the other patrons would have gotten an eyeful.

Marcus removed his finger and traced the outline of her lips. He pushed her wineglass in front of her.

"Drink, then lick your lips. Taste how fucking sweet you are mixed with the wine."

Carrie drank the wine and tasted her own arousal. She was drowning in the sensation. She felt so empty, bereft, needing to be filled. As though he could read her mind, she felt something hard and cool slide between her nether lips. Marcus pushed the hidden object deep within her. She sucked in a breath when, a mere second later, it started to vibrate very softly inside of her.

"Oh, God," she whispered. There was no way she could sit there and not orgasm.

When she started to move slightly, the vibration stopped. Her cry of disappointment slipped out before she could stop herself.

"Every time you move I'll stop the vibrator."

She put every ounce of pleading she could into her eyes as she looked at him but Marcus wouldn't relent.

"We are going to sit here and enjoy a great dinner. You're going to answer all my questions, tell me everything about you, and you're not going to come. This is your first punishment, Carrie."

He flipped the vibe back on.

Chapter Seven

୨୦

Carrie squeezed her thighs together, trying her damnedest to stem the clenching of her muscles. They were in constant tremor. Marcus obviously took great pleasure in increasing or decreasing the vibrations. There was no rhyme or reason, just when he felt like driving her crazy beyond anything.

She became oblivious to her surroundings. For Carrie, there were no other patrons, no waitstaff. Only she and Marcus occupied the space of the restaurant.

"So, when is the baby due?" Marcus asked as he poured them another glass of wine. After their food had arrived, he'd begun to question Carrie about her life, her education, her family. She'd opened up to him about it all. He was interested and curious, laughing easily. He was unguarded for once, a sight Carrie rarely witnessed. It felt like a regular date. Regular, that is, until he turned the infernal vibe off or on.

"Officially not for two more weeks but the doctor told her it could be sooner."

She felt so bad for her younger sister. Cassidy had married Kevin Lassiter after a whirlwind courtship and surprise pregnancy. Then he was shipped off to Iraq where a roadside bomb killed him a mere two weeks after his unit arrived.

Cass had been thrown for a loop, left alone pregnant and a widow.

"My parents are with her now. Luckily, Chicago is just a forty-five minute flight. I was planning on going out there in ten days and staying until she has the baby."

The waitress took their empty plates away and brought dessert. Carrie eyed the plain vanilla ice cream and laughed. Marcus was many things but plain vanilla wasn't one of them.

He noticed the odd expression on her face and, dipping one finger into the icy confection, he slid his ice-cream-coated finger across her bottom lip. Smearing it, he leaned in and licked it off.

"Ever play with your food, Carrie?" he whispered in her ear. He presented his finger again, full of ice cream. "Suck it off."

She closed her eyes and opened her mouth.

"No, I want your eyes open and on me. Always on me," he grumbled. She opened her eyes and he slid his finger into her mouth.

Who knew that sucking a finger could be such an erotic experience?

"Suck it like it's my cock, baby."

Carrie pulled him in deeply, watching gray eyes go silver with every stroke of her tongue.

Marcus pulled his finger out and repeated the process several times, feeding her the sweet dessert. When they were down to almost the bottom of the bowl, he changed tactics.

Instead of his finger going to her mouth, it traveled under the table, the cold cream touching hot, weepy flesh between her thighs. Carrie was unable to stop her gasp at the contact. Marcus pulled the vibe from her, replacing it with his cold finger. Taking it back out, he gathered the last of the vanilla treat. Sliding his hand back under her skirt, he surrounded her clit, rubbing it slowly. She shuddered under the lick of pleasure/pain as her clit went numb.

"Stand up and go to the ladies' room. Take off your panties and sit down on the couch, legs spread, skirt up. Wait for me there."

Carrie looked at him. Was he serious? His expression told her that he was. She left the safety of the booth and made her way to the restroom.

Marcus didn't keep her waiting long; he had a quiet word with Joseph, the restaurant's owner, and then joined her.

She was sitting exactly as he'd instructed, perched on the couch, her skirt hiked to the tops of her thighs, lace-edged stockings showing. Marcus didn't even pretend to lock the door. He knew that Joseph would take care of anyone wanting to enter this particular room until they were through.

Marcus didn't tell Carrie that, though. It was important that she trust him enough to know he wouldn't put her in a position to cause her any embarrassment.

She was nervous, looking everywhere but directly at him. He walked over to her and went to his knees. Placing a hand on each of her ankles, he slowly let his palms ride up the silky stockings.

"Carrie. Where should your eyes be?" He kept his voice soft but he could see his words flash through her like lightning as her eyes whipped to his face. "Oh, you are just piling up the punishments." He tried to sound regretful as she shuddered but truthfully, he could hardly wait to have her tied and vulnerable, waiting for his discipline.

"Now, reach above your head and grab the back of the couch." He waited until she'd complied. "Do not remove them."

She gave a jerky nod. Her chest heaved with each breath.

Marcus had a hand on each knee and he pushed them as far apart as the skirt of her dress would allow.

"Keep very still. I don't want to be disturbed while I'm eating my dessert." He wasn't able to keep the wicked grin off of his face and was delighted with her gasp.

She made him feel powerful and he wanted nothing more than to please her body. Put his permanent stamp upon her.

He looked down at her plump nether lips. They glistened with arousal and melted, sticky ice cream. He leaned in. Placing his tongue on her smooth skin, he licked off every bit of the ice cream he'd put on her flesh. The taste was intoxicating, Carrie's sweet juices combined with the rich treat. His mouth and tongue played over the outer skin until, finally unable to stand another second, he brought his thumbs up, pulling her apart.

Marcus' breath caught at the sight. She was so fucking turned on. Man, he couldn't remember a woman ever being this wet for him. His tongue was greedy as he moved forward and lapped her pussy.

He took turns rimming her entrance then pushing in. He sucked the combined cream from her body. Small amounts had dripped down farther, landing on her most secret of holes, and Marcus licked her there as well. Her cries were muted as she tried to remain still and not bring in unwanted attention to the room they were in.

Carrie's head fell back as Marcus speared her again with his tongue. No man had ever treated her like dessert. Marcus drank nosily from between her thighs. She moaned louder now as he slipped two fingers into her channel. Crooking them, he moved them around until she cried out. He zeroed in on the exact location of her G-spot. Carrie was ready to fall to pieces as his sure fingers stroked her steadily, building up her pleasure.

"Marcus, please," she sobbed. She may be embarrassed later at how needy she sounded, but not now. Now she needed to come in his mouth.

"Please what, baby? And look at me when you ask." The smooth cadence of his voice bathed her in desire.

She met his eyes, which mirrored the passion she was sure showed in her own.

"Please, Marcus, I need to come."

He smiled at her before diving back between her thighs and working her clit into his mouth. He sucked hard, nibbling it before soothing it with his tongue.

He pulled back just enough to say, "You've been a bad girl today. I shouldn't let you."

Her whimper of distress came out perilously like a sob.

He flicked his tongue over her clit once more before murmuring into her pulsing flesh, "Then come for me, baby."

Her body immediately convulsed around his fingers, clutching them tightly inside as Carrie let loose a sound she'd never have recognized as coming from her own mouth. She shivered and shook endlessly, riding out the absolute, most pleasurable feeling she'd ever known.

Marcus slowly withdrew from her and she felt empty, but he didn't give her long to mourn the loss of his touch. He rose, grabbing the back of her hair and pulling until she looked up into his eyes.

"You're so beautiful when you come for me," he said and claimed her mouth with a kiss that burned her from head to toe. He was declaring ownership. Carrie kissed him back, trying to demand the same thing from him.

God, she was in over her head. How the hell was life supposed to continue as it had been when this weekend was over? She was headed for the worst kind of heartbreak but she was unable to tear herself away from him. She would worry about the rest later.

"I need to hold you." Her voice was a raw whisper, strained from her screams.

"Then hold me," Marcus responded against her lips.

Wrapping her arms around his back, she pulled him closer as they kissed over and over until they had to break apart to breathe, both panting heavily.

Marcus stood, not meeting her eyes. He carefully helped Carrie to her feet.

"Let's go home," was all he said as he opened the door and escorted her out.

Chapter Eight

ഔ

They rode back to Marcus' house in silence. In fact, the only movement had been when Marcus placed Carrie's hand over his thigh and squeezed it. She kept it on his firm muscle until they pulled back into his driveway.

He came around to her side of the car, helping her out, leading her back into his house.

After closing the door, he guided Carrie up the stairs to the back of the house. There he unlocked a simple door, escorting her inside. Marcus turned on the light, which bathed the room in a soft glow.

The walls here were a deep scarlet, so unlike the stark white rooms downstairs. Rooms that held the barest amount of furniture. There were no family photos, nothing to personalize his living space. It was as though he never spent time in his house. It was hard to call such a cold place home. *Unfinished* was how Carrie thought of it. So unlike her own cozy apartment, which was brightly colored and full of her personal photos and souvenirs.

She examined the contents of the scarlet room, noting all the equipment, and gaped. In the corner was a low bed. Several steel bars were placed at varying heights around the room. A large X covered in black leather leaned slightly against one wall.

A black, fur-covered, gymnastic-style horse stood ominously near the bed. On the other side of the bed, a large armoire loomed, doors slightly ajar. Inside, she saw paddles, floggers and a multitude of other implements she couldn't even begin to name. Set inside as well was a vertical row of small pull-out drawers. She shivered when she tried to imagine all the toys that might be hidden there.

Square in the middle of the room sat the most interesting structure: one large step flanked on either side by two smaller steps, almost like the winner's podium at the Olympics. Above the top step hung a large gold ring. It didn't take a genius to understand what was supposed to hang from the ring.

Anticipation slithered down Carrie's spine, along with a healthy dose of caution, as she fantasized about each item.

Marcus left her in the middle of the room and took a seat in a leather wingback chair, appearing completely content to watch her take in the sights. He looked so relaxed, so comfortable. This was his domain, and his obvious ease with the room radiated from him. He was in his element and it showed on his handsome face.

"You did well at the restaurant."

She cast her eyes down as he spoke.

"Carrie." His voice was much harsher this time. "You will not look away or down from me, ever. You are to keep your eyes on me always. I want a submissive, not a slave, and as such it's important that I am always able to see your reaction."

When he spoke, she snapped to attention and those beautiful brown eyes gazed straight at him. Carrie had no clue how important it was to him that she always meet his eyes.

While it was true that he wasn't looking for a slave and that he needed to gauge her reactions, his need for her attention went much deeper.

Karen had never met his eyes. With Carrie it had to be different. He felt it deep in his bones. His reaction to her being here, in his home, stirred up feelings he wasn't prepared to deal with. So rather than try to analyze his own reactions, he was determined to examine every facet of hers.

"Now strip." He watched intently as she slipped her filmy black dress over her head. She stood tall and proud before him, her brand-new scarlet lace bra and matching panties exquisite against her pale skin.

Fuck, she was beautiful, her full breasts stretching the lacy bra. Marcus' cock pushed hard against the denim of his pants, like it wanted to reach out and stake a claim on this woman. He breathed in deeply, trying to get himself under control. Carrie's beautiful, curvaceous body was making that impossible.

"Turn around and bend over for me." Marcus' voice was slightly husky this time as she turned around and bent at the waist.

His palms throbbed with the need to touch her. Standing up, he eased himself over to her, placing both palms against her ass and massaging the firm flesh deeply. Closing his eyes, he rubbed her dewy, soft skin before slowly circling back and forth. He stepped back and pulled a chair around to stand in front of her.

"Hold onto the chair. It's time for the rest of your punishment."

She immediately complied, which brought a smile to Marcus' face. He slid her panties down to her knees.

"Spread your legs as wide as you can, baby," he whispered, watching in fascination as she widened her stance. His mouth watered at the sight of the red lace tight around her knees, her ass on display for him.

Marcus placed both hands against her bare ass. Rubbing lightly, he skimmed the surface with the tips of his fingers. When he noticed her legs getting restless, he slid a finger along her slit.

Marcus marched his fingers to her hard little clit, placing the very tip of one directly below it. He traced circles around it, not quite touching but causing all kinds of sensations to run through her body, as were evidenced by the multitude of goose bumps along her skin.

"You were a very bad girl today," he murmured and then smacked her behind. It was more noise than anything else but she jumped, a tiny squeak slipping from between her closed lips. Marcus grinned when her skin became pink with his handprint. It looked perfect there, marking her ass as his.

"You aren't allowed to come ever, baby, not unless I give you permission." Again he landed another blow in a different spot.

"Do you understand what I am saying to you?" Another spank. Pushing two fingers into her wet entrance, he gave her three more slaps to her ass. She was soaking his hand and Marcus loved it. He wanted her opened wide and dripping and he really fucking wanted to lick her clean.

He slowly inserted a third finger. It glided effortlessly in and out of her swollen passage. He landed another stinging slap while increasing the speed of his fingers pumping her. She was so close to coming.

"Tell me what you can't do."

When she hesitated, panting, he landed another smack. Her skin became red faster this time.

"Come," she half sobbed. "I can't come until you say I can. Marcus!" She cried out as he shoved his fingers more forcefully into her.

He leaned over and kissed the middle of her spine.

"Good girl," he whispered against her back.

His desire for her was like a fire that couldn't be quenched. Marcus feared in that moment that he would never get enough of Carrie, never tire of her.

When his thoughts began straying into territory he didn't want to deal with, he brought his shaking hand to his lips. Humming his enjoyment, he licked her sweet juice from his fingers. She tasted like the sweetest peach, and he savored the unique flavor of her essence.

Walking over to the armoire, he pulled open a drawer. Inside were two boxes, one white, one black. He chose the black one and, moving back to her, he stood behind her.

"Turn around."

She turned to face him. She was flushed; her dark brown eyes were glazed. Marcus imagined what her reaction would be when he was buried deep inside of her welcoming, plush body. His cock, jerking in his pants again, reminded him that time was a-wasting.

Marcus opened the long box and withdrew a red velvet collar. It was plain but laden with meaning. He'd picked it especially for her, knowing how the deep scarlet color would contrast with her smooth, pale skin and dark hair and eyes.

"Carrie, will you wear my collar this weekend? It's my gift to you."

Her eyes shone brightly, as though he were offering her diamonds instead of plain velvet.

"Oh yes, Marcus, I will."

Her words struck him with the force of a vow. Without the slightest hesitation, she turned back around and lifted her hair that he could place the strap around her neck.

Karen had allowed him to collar her once and then she'd insisted it be made of nothing but diamonds. His ex would have laughed her ass off to receive such a simple gift. Carrie had amazed him again. The differences between her and Karen had always been there but they had never been more pronounced than they were in this moment.

He carefully clasped the collar into place. It was a perfect fit. A small length of silver chain dangled from the clasp, emphasizing the delicacy of her neck. Stepping in front of her, Marcus held back a smile at the wonder in her expression. He needed to play this cool.

She absently stroked the collar, her body visibly trembling with frustrated arousal.

"Take off your panties and assume your position." He watched with satisfaction as she shimmied out of her panties and dropped to her knees before him, holding her scarlet-lace-clad breasts up to him like a gift. He stepped close to her and murmured, "Put your mouth on my cock. Make me feel it through my pants."

She immediately complied, opening those luscious lips over the throbbing bar of his cock. The pleasure was maddening, even muted through the fabric of his jeans.

"Go to the cross," he said, pointing to the X-frame. "And crawl. I want to see that gorgeous ass sway."

Her eyes sparked with anxiety and desire as she crawled like a jungle cat in heat across the floor, her curves and her skin so fucking sweet. He smiled in approval when she reached the apparatus and automatically resumed her position.

"Stand up, baby. I want you stretched out on the cross for me."

She moved gracefully and obediently, her gaze never leaving his.

By the end of the weekend, Marcus was certain that she would belong to him. In fact, he suspected she already did. The question remained, was Marcus ready for it? There was something more here than fulfilling his ex-assistant's fantasy of being dominated or his desire for her tender body. He knew his heart was dangerously close to giving in to the feelings he'd hoarded for her over the years. Feelings he'd always refused to put a name to. Feelings he'd always put off as caused by the fact that they'd worked so closely together for so long, that she'd been there for him when no one else had.

Tonight he wasn't using that excuse. Marcus wasn't a fool. He knew that this weekend would plot the course of his future. And he prayed it would turn out better than the past had.

Fuck, he was turning into a sappy ass again. Daniel was never going to let him live this down.

Carrie stepped up to the leather-bound contraption and stopped, waiting for further instructions. The collar felt soft against her throat, and as she stroked the lush fabric it made her feel like a princess. This collar would always serve as a reminder of her weekend with Marcus Worthington. If their relationship didn't go beyond the next few days, she would have this to remember the best time of her life. A time when she felt beautiful, wanted and needed by the man she loved.

"Place your back against the X and raise your arms above your head," Marcus murmured into her ear. While he kept the volume soft, the tone was commanding, and she shivered. She stepped onto the small platform and raised her arms.

Marcus reached up and placed one wrist into a leather cuff, securing it snugly enough to restrain her but not tight enough to hurt. He then moved to her elbow, repeating the procedure. He cuffed her other arm in the same fashion, leaving her upper body completely immobilized against the apparatus. The cool leather felt wonderful next to her heated skin.

Carrie stood before him, her breasts thrust outward, begging for his attention. Her ass was pushed tight against the leather.

He skimmed over the cups of her bra, tracing patterns over the lace before cupping her breasts and palming them as her nipples stiffened and thrust out. His steely gray eyes never leaving hers, he grabbed the middle of the bra and ripped it in two. Carrie's breasts spilled out, and he hissed loudly as he let one finger trace the valley between her breasts before stroking it over the full mound.

He let his finger slide over to her left nipple. Placing the pad of his finger on it, he moved it in circles before plucking lightly at the rosy bud and pulling it away taut. She closed her eyes and focused on the sheer pleasure he was giving her with his touch.

"Carrie," he warned. "Open your eyes."

She snapped her lids up and watched him as he licked his finger and thumb, grasping her other nipple. Her nipples stretched and elongated with every flick of his skillful fingers.

"Damn, baby, your nipples are so responsive." He leaned forward and wrapped his lips around one stiff peak, sucking it deeply into his mouth, grazing his teeth across it. The pleasure centering in her nipple shot straight to her pussy. Her arousal starting to coat her lower lips, she couldn't hold back and let out a small, breathless moan.

"That's it, baby. Cry out when it feels good." His lips went back to her chest, giving her other nipple the same careful attention as the first.

"These would look so fucking beautiful with a hoop through them." Marcus emphasized his point by pinching the tight tips. "So long, so fucking hot."

His head ducked to lick, suck and nibble at her breasts some more. He played with her until the liquid between her legs began traveling down the tops of her thighs. Carrie's body was strung so tightly she knew Marcus could make her come instantly with one touch. She was already on fire from the spanking. Now he was turning up the heat with his careful ministrations to her breasts.

He licked down between her breasts, making appreciative noises that vibrated against her skin. There wasn't an area on her upper torso that he didn't brand with his mouth, lips or tongue.

He slipped down to her navel, kissing the skin surrounding the soft indention. He dragged his teeth along her lower tummy, scraping her heaving flesh. She wriggled mindlessly, trying to grind herself against him.

Marcus lifted one of her feet and placed it at one end of the platform. He cuffed her ankle in the same manner as he had her wrists, and cuffed her again at the knee. Pulling her other leg to the opposite end of the platform, he cuffed that one as well.

Now she was opened wide for his view. She couldn't move, couldn't do more than squirm and watch him glide around her. He was graceful, like a wild animal on the prowl, his muscles bunching underneath his shirt, his ebony hair shining blue-black beneath the soft light in the room, his skin golden from playing outdoors in the summer sun.

Some would say that his face was a little too harsh to be considered truly handsome, that he lacked beauty though he had character and strength. Carrie couldn't disagree more. To her, Marcus was the most beautiful man in the world. In the office it had been so difficult to tear her gaze away from him as they worked together. He was strong, and smart and arrogant when it came to business matters. In her eyes, he was sheer perfection.

There were other sides to him as well, though he rarely showed them. Sides she'd only glimpsed now and then. There was his helpless tenderness for his sister. His amused indulgence of his brother. The way he so ardently supported local law enforcement and rescue services. So many facets to this beautiful, complex man. How could she help but to love him?

"Arch your back for me." Marcus' voice ripped her thoughts back to the present. She arched as far as she could comfortably go. The position opened her up wider, put her on display for his avid gaze.

He slipped a finger inside her labia, pressing slowly along her slit. Carrie moaned at the invasion of his thick finger. Her muscles clenched as he pressed into her entrance.

Marcus leaned forward and inhaled deeply, rumbling his approval in his chest. His tongue came out and stroked her quivering lips.

"Oh God," she sobbed as he ran his tongue around her clit. Wrapping his lips around her hard cherry, he pulled it between his lips, licking and sucking until she was grinding helplessly down against his face. She wanted to feel every part of his mouth on her.

He tongued her from clit to opening, swirling around her soaked entrance before entering. She was bound helplessly, trying to stave off her impending orgasm while he fucked her with his wickedly long tongue, stabbing into her, lapping at her cream. She was on the edge, teetering between heaven and hell. Was Marcus her angel or demon? She was debating the issue when he suddenly pulled his mouth away from her.

"Carrie, are you on the Pill?" Marcus managed to grit the words out between clenched teeth. Had he lost his damn mind? Marcus hadn't had unprotected sex since his divorce. In fact he'd rarely even had it during his marriage. Karen hadn't liked the mess. He was diligent about getting tested but only because he believed safety to be one of the most important and responsible things in life, not because he planned to fuck bare.

Now he was hoping against hope that she *was* protected so that he could drive into her with no barriers. His hand moved between her legs to tease her some more. Her lips were plump and pink and glistening with her arousal. He stroked her outer labia, enjoying the fact that she shaved. He was going to change that; shaving was ok but she would be getting waxed for him from now on.

"Answer me, baby. Are you on the Pill?"

"Yes." Her brown eyes, so wide and desperate, locked helplessly on his.

"Carrie, this is up to you. But, fuck, I want to be in you bareback. I want to feel you squeeze every little drop out of me. I'm completely healthy. I would never put you in any kind of danger. If you aren't comfortable, I can use something. Either way, I'm okay with it."

Something akin to wonder lit her face as she softly answered him.

"I trust you, Marcus. And I want to feel you come inside me." The haze in her eyes cleared slightly. "Shouldn't you be asking if *I'm* clean?"

"Baby," he growled against her lips, "you are the purest thing I've ever touched."

His answer seemed to please her. She gave that secret little smile and said, "I want you to fuck me bare, Marcus. Please put me out of my misery."

Her words shot down his spine like lightning, searing him from nape to groin. It was all he needed to hear, and he threw off his shirt and pushed down his pants. He stepped up to his woman, for in his soul he knew that Carrie *was* his woman, and trembled as he placed his cock to her pussy.

He leaned forward until their noses were almost touching. Her breath bathed his face in anticipation.

Marcus bent briefly and freed her legs. He placed one hand at the back of her head. Wrapping his fingers in her hair, he pulled back slightly, forcing her to meet his eyes. And then he thrust home.

Chapter Nine

ॐ

"Fuck, Carrie." They were the only words Marcus could get past his throat; it had closed up on him as he tunneled through her wet heat. She was tight around his cock but so slick he was able to move in and out of her easily. Without the barrier of a condom, he felt like he was in free fall. He pulled one of her legs up over his thigh and she finished the job by wrapping it around his hip. He kept his movements slow and steady. Marcus wanted to draw out the pleasure for her, and for himself.

Her feel, her taste, her smell, everything about her was total perfection wrapped in a stunningly curvy body. He raised her other leg, sliding it around his body while his elbows went under each knee. He widened her and drove himself that much deeper into her warm recesses. He tilted his upper body back, aligning his cock with the spongy tissue deep within her. Her eyes went wide as he dragged his cock back and forth over the slight swelling. Her face was awash with astonishment as new sensations of utter delight burst through her body. Marcus was so proud of her and so turned on. He knew she was trying desperately to hold back her orgasm.

He rammed into her like a man possessed. He found her full ass and clutched the supple skin tightly, holding on for dear life. He felt like if he let go, he'd fly into a million pieces.

He latched onto the side of her neck, just above the collar, and bit down. A squeal of pure bliss rushed from her lips. Marcus licked the area; he knew his mark would still be there in the morning. It sent a thrill climbing up his spine. His body was in perfect tune with hers. Carrie's muscles pulsed tightly around his heavy cock. Fuck, he was so ready to let go.

Fighting it with every pump of his hips, he curled one hand gently around the front of her throat, his thumb rubbing back and forth along her chin. Her small pink tongue darted from her mouth, licking her parched lips, tempting him beyond bearing.

He groaned and slid his thumb into her mouth. She sucked it hard, just like she had sucked his dick.

Her mouth was more than he could stand. He placed his forehead against hers.

"Come for me, Carrie. Come now!" His roar bounced off the walls. Her legs writhed, her feet dug into his back, her big chocolate eyes went wild with the force of her orgasm. Driving into her welcoming heat, he went up in flames as her sweet juice coated his cock.

Marcus quickly followed her into oblivion as he released his come into her waiting womb. He pumped into her endlessly, amazed at his body's ability to keep shooting into her.

When he was sure he couldn't spill another drop, he let go of her legs. Quickly, he reached up and freed her wrists.

Carrie collapsed into his arms, unable to form a coherent thought much less move her limbs voluntarily. Her body, jumping with the aftershocks of the most intense orgasm of her life, seemed totally out of her control. She hadn't known it was possible to feel such an overwhelming sense of fulfillment.

Marcus gently drew her away from the cross and over to the bed. He laid her down and crawled in beside her.

He cupped her face and stroked his thumb back and forth across her cheek. It was such a simple act but it made her feel warm and safe. No words were needed during these moments. In fact, Carrie didn't want any words. She wanted to bask in the fantasy that he loved her.

Eventually he tucked her into his side, rubbing her back and lulling her. She stifled a yawn but Marcus caught it and chuckled. "Close your eyes and get some rest, baby. You're going to need it."

* * * * *

Carrie was awakened sometime later by Marcus' mouth drifting down the column of her throat.

"How are you feeling?" His voice was rough with sleep and sex.

She smiled. "I feel wonderful."

He propped his head in his palm, facing her. He drew patterns along the side of her upper thighs. His erection pressed into her ribs. Carrie's temperature rose several degrees as his strokes became more forceful. He glided his hand to her ass and squeezed the plump cheek.

"Do you trust me?" His face was blank of emotion as he asked.

"Of course I do." Wasn't this whole weekend about trust?

Seeming satisfied with her answer, he leaned over and brushed a kiss to her forehead.

"Go into the bathroom and take a shower. There is a razor in the shower. I want that pussy as bare and silky as satin. There are several lotions. Choose whichever you like and rub it slowly over your entire body." He smiled into her slumberous eyes. "What will you *not* do?"

"I won't make myself come," she breathed back to him.

"Excellent. When you're done, come back to me."

She rolled over and her well-used muscles protested when she finally rose from the bed. The hot shower sounded heavenly as she swayed into the little bathroom. Looking over her shoulder to gauge Marcus' reaction to her little hip sway, she couldn't help but grin. His eyes could have melted steel, they burned so brightly.

The door to the playroom opened and Daniel Ellis sauntered through. He was dressed in leather pants and a blue silk shirt the same color as his eyes. Daniel loved silk.

Marcus sat up. He'd taken his shower before waking Carrie, and now he tightened the towel hanging low on his hips.

Daniel unbuttoned his shirt, beginning with the cuffs at each wrist.

"Well, don't keep me in suspense. How's it going?" He had a stupid-ass grin on his face like he knew something Marcus didn't. And it irritated the hell out of Marcus.

"How do you think it's going? She's doing well."

A blond eyebrow shot up. "She's doing well? Damn. Is that all you have to say?"

Marc stood and paced in front of his bed. "What exactly should I be telling you, Daniel? You're going to experience her for yourself."

He stopped when he felt Daniel's hand on his shoulder.

"Hey, we don't have to go through with this. It's not too late for me to leave. She'll never even know I was here. No harm, no foul."

Marcus caught his best friend's eyes. "I have to. I need to. I can't explain it any better than that."

Daniel sighed. He knew exactly why Marcus needed this, and he hated that The Viper had used him as her weapon against his best friend.

"Marcus, I don't want this to come between us. After the number Kar…"

"Don't fucking bring her name up tonight. This is completely different."

Daniel nodded and continued at his buttons but he wasn't convinced. It had taken a long time for him and Marc to get past the awkwardness of Karen's betrayal, and Daniel had an idea that if things went badly with Carrie, their friendship would never recover.

The sound of the shower stopped and Marcus' gaze snapped eagerly to the doorway. Daniel rubbed his chin as he kept an eye on his best friend. Marcus was so totally screwed. It was hard for him not to laugh out loud. He could see what Marcus was refusing to acknowledge.

The evil side of Daniel decided that tonight he would prove just how nuts his best friend really was for Carrie. While he knew he'd never experience what Marcus was so obviously feeling, he wasn't opposed to pushing his best friend. Marcus loved this woman. Daniel was no expert on the subject but the look in Marcus' eyes told him all he needed to know.

For the first time in the course of their friendship, Marcus didn't want to share. Oh, he may be putting up a good front but anyone with eyes could see the strain he was trying to hide. Understanding all the dynamics at work here, Daniel should have felt like he was being used. Instead he felt almost honored. How Carrie responded to their time together might give Marcus the small push he needed back into the world of the living.

Since the divorce, the Old Man's death, Marcus had changed. No more easy smile, no laughing and joking. Nothing but his guilt over the past, which was so great that he wore it like a giant shroud. A shroud he used to push everyone away, including those in his inner circle.

As Marcus had rushed deeper and darker into himself, dammit, Daniel had been worried. Worried right up until the moment Carrie approached him about joining the club. Marcus' reaction to seeing her at Velvet Ice only confirmed what he already knew.

He wanted his best friend happy. Hell, someone deserved that kind of happiness, Marcus more so than most.

Marcus and Carrie belonged together. True, she wasn't like his usual women. That alone made her special. The fact that she'd stood by Marcus through all the shit had earned Daniel's respect. If he'd been the kind of man who could settle down, he may have made a play for the woman himself.

Not that it would have worked. Whenever Carrie looked at Marcus, her desire was stamped all over her face. She wanted to belong to him, she wanted to love him. That she'd agreed to this weekend with Marcus only endeared her more to Daniel. She was fighting for Marcus, fighting for a future with him.

Well, tonight Daniel was going to make sure Marcus and Carrie came out of this weekend together, even if it meant pissing off his best friend in the process. Hell, he grinned, especially if it meant pissing off his best friend in the process.

When Carrie opened the bathroom door, Marcus was waiting for her, immediately wrapping a black scarf across her eyes. She loved the sensation of being totally dependent on him to guide her through the room. Marcus kept her constantly on edge, her body teetering on the precipice of a desire so deep that it scared the hell out of her.

"You trust me?" Again he asked the question.

"Marcus, didn't we already go through this?" She wasn't sure why he needed her to repeat her answer.

A stinging slap hit her behind and she yelped but couldn't keep the smile from her face. She liked the way her cheeks warmed and how it seemed to be a direct line to her pussy. A signal for her body to soften for what was to come.

"Don't get smart or I'll have to spank you." He tried to sound stern but Carrie could hear the amusement in his voice.

Still smiling, she murmured, "That's not much of an incentive for me to behave." She savored his rough laugh.

"I have a surprise for you," he whispered as he led her through the room and lifted her to stand on a platform. "Assume your position."

She immediately sank to her knees, opening her legs wide and clutching her heavy breasts to present to Marcus.

He walked up behind her and stroked the long line of her spine.

"Remember, Carrie-mine, we can stop at any time. I would never hurt you."

An involuntary shudder went through her at his intimately whispered words. The pain was almost as strong as the arousal. She wished he really meant it when he called her his. She felt his mouth at her nape and leaned into the kiss.

Chapter Ten

ം

A second pair of hands touched her just underneath her breasts. She froze as the second person in the room spoke.

"Damn, Marcus, she really is beautiful."

Carrie couldn't move. That voice. She'd know that smooth cadence anywhere.

Marcus grabbed her hips and rocked against her backside. "Yes, she's quite the beauty."

She gasped at the compliments and turned red. "Okay, guys, you're laying it on a little thick."

Teeth closed over her shoulder and bit hard.

"Daniel, I think we need to explain to Carrie what really counts as beautiful."

She felt Daniel's smooth chuckle against her face. "I agree. And remind her that a good little submissive doesn't speak until spoken to." His velvet-smooth tongue licked down her nose, across her cheeks. He nipped sharply at her chin before rising to kiss her temples.

"True beauty lies in here," he said as his hands ran down the sides of her face, stroking hair. Daniel's mouth whispered lightly across her head. "It lies here." His finger touching the shell of her ear before licking the highly charged spot. "It lies here," he finished as his flat palm slid down her sternum to rest in the valley of her breasts.

"You're gorgeous, Carrie, because you understand what we want. What we need you to do. Baby, you are the most sensual creature I have ever known." She imagined Daniel was smirking a little bit while Marcus glared at him and growled.

Carrie sighed as Marcus bit her earlobe. Daniel's compliment pierced her heart. No man had ever told her she was beautiful, and now two of the hottest men in Detroit were showering her with praise. The only thing that could have made it better was if the words had come from Marcus himself.

"Of course we can't forget about this body," Daniel said as he cupped each of her breasts. She could practically *hear* him smiling. "Told ya I like them juicy."

Carrie stifled a giggle as Marcus growled into the back of her neck.

"You are perfect just as you are, kneeling obediently before me. And I want you so fucking bad I can't stand it." Marcus' confession brought tears to Carrie's eyes, dampening the black silk scarf.

She felt Daniel's heat as it blanketed the front of her.

"Marcus is damn lucky he got to you first." He pressed firm lips to hers. Slowly, taking his time, he covered Carrie's face with soft butterfly kisses. Marcus was at her back, licking her neck. The sensations were tremendous, as her entire upper body was enveloped in heat.

"On the bench. Lay down on your back." Marcus led her toward the bench. Her back sank into the softest leather that molded to her skin. She was grateful for the blindfold. She didn't know if she could bear to face the two men as they approached her. When they stood on either side of the bench, she realized that, if she remembered correctly, it was the perfect height to take one of them in her mouth and the other in her pussy.

She squeezed her thighs together as the image of Daniel sliding his long, hard cock between her lips while Marcus pumped into her crashed into her brain.

"Arms up, Carrie-mine."

She followed his command easily as the anticipation of the pleasure to come buzzed around in her brain, shooting signals to other, and more intimate, parts of her body.

Some tiny voice whispered that she shouldn't want this, to be shared by the man she loved. Carrie ignored it. There was no *should* or *shouldn't* in this situation. She wanted Marcus' possession. If this weekend was all she would have of Marcus' domination, then she was determined to give him everything he asked for.

And honestly, being with Daniel was no hardship. The man might have shadows in his eyes that would make the boldest lover cautious but he was still one of the most beautiful men she'd ever seen, and he'd already proven his touch could set her body alight.

Two sets of hands restrained her wrists, fastening them with leather straps to the bench. The straps were tight, leaving no wiggle room for her upper body unless she scooted up.

She turned her head, following the sound of Marcus' footsteps as he went over to his toy chest. She heard drawers opening and closing and pictured him pulling out a variety of toys. The thought of him using them on her sent hot cream sliding down her thighs.

He returned to the bench and knelt down. "Carrie, you are to listen to Daniel's instructions as if they were my own, do you understand?"

She couldn't find her voice but she managed to nod her head. Blinded by the black silk, she had no warning. Suddenly two sets of lips descended on her nipples.

"Oh, God," she croaked as the sensation of two very different tongues began licking at the taut buds. Each man played with them in different ways, eliciting duel reactions of pleasure from her. She wasn't able to concentrate on either man, only on the sensations they were driving into her chest and throughout the rest of her body.

Marcus pulled Carrie's nipple deep into his mouth, flicking it back and forth. Catching it in a gentle grip with his teeth, he pulled, elongating it as much as possible. Her head thrashed back and forth and small whimpers escaped with each pull.

His eyes cut across to Daniel, who was moaning as he swirled his tongue around her entire breast. He was devouring her, enjoying himself just a little too much for Marcus' peace of mind. What the hell kind of game was Danny-boy playing? If he wanted to piss Marcus off, he was well on the way to succeeding.

When he recognized his irrational possessiveness, he knew it was time to take the next step. Without releasing her painfully hard nipple, Marcus reached up and untied the blindfold. He slowly slid the silk away, letting the fabric drag over her damp, flushed skin. Her eyes were closed, her lips parted on gasping breaths as her head thrashed against the warm leather of the bench.

He bit down harder. "Keep your eyes open, Carrie," he reprimanded her and then went back to tormenting her tender nipple. He fucking loved the taste of her skin. So smooth, so sweetly Carrie.

Marcus brought his eyes back to Carrie's and wanted to moan as he encountered those dark brown orbs fixed on the sight of his mouth on her body.

"She's ready," Marcus rasped as he broke contact. He picked up the clamps that he'd placed on the carpet beside the bench, ready to give one to Daniel. His friend still had his lips wrapped firmly around Carrie's nipple, drawing moans of pleasure from her with each suck.

"*Dan.*" Marcus didn't raise his voice but the words rapped out with unmistakable demand. Daniel let go slowly with a small pop as her nipple slid free. Silently, Marcus handed over the clamp.

Carrie's eyes widened at the sight of them. Marcus leaned down and pulled her nipple between his fingers, twisting gently. Daniel followed suit and, with a look to coordinate their timing, they each let a clamp bite into her tender flesh.

Marcus quickly placed his mouth over Carrie's, inhaling her cry at the sharp bite of pain. Daniel was whispering in her ear, sweet words telling her how the pain would dwindle in a moment, and for her to hold on, the pleasure would be more than she had ever imagined. Marcus' tongue slid deeper into her mouth, thrusting and stroking until her cries ended and her tongue began dancing with his own.

Breaking the kiss, he looked over at his best friend. He hoped Daniel would never know what the words cost him as he said, "Well, you're the guest. Where would you like to start?"

He didn't like the wolfish grin that spread across Daniel's face.

"Hey, don't I get a say?" Her small voice broke the tension between him and Daniel.

"Are you questioning me, Carrie?" She met the silver fire in his eyes and shook her head frantically. "No, you don't get a say," he answered. "You know what to say if you want out."

He reminded her of the safe word they'd agreed upon earlier. When he'd asked her for one, she'd opened her mouth and out came the word *apple*. He was amused as she blushed over the silly word. Maybe she thought it should have been something more interesting or dignified. He'd wanted to reassure that most times the word was kept simple, easy to remember in the heat of passion. Instead Marcus had simply grinned and nodded his agreement. Apple was the safe word. She only had to say it, and Marcus would untie her and kick Daniel's conceited ass out of here.

"Since you haven't said that word," he flicked at her adorned nipple. "I'll assume you don't want to stop."

"No, I don't want to stop," she replied, her cheeks stained pink with a flush of embarrassment and arousal.

"Then baby, you're racking up the punishments."

"Well then," Daniel said, standing up and going to the bottom of the bench. "If we're done with all the conversation, I'm hungry and I think I would like to eat some dessert."

He grasped each of Carrie's legs and positioned them over his shoulders. Marcus watched as his best friend split Carrie's glossy, swollen pussy lips apart like a piece of succulent fruit, dragging his tongue up the tender slit in one long stroke.

He was turned on and pissed off all at the same time. Marcus hadn't seen Daniel this eager to dive between a woman's legs in quite a while and he didn't particularly like that it was *his* woman who had inspired Daniel's enthusiasm.

Turning back to Carrie, he had to resist the sudden urge to cover her, take her and make her his alone. Even though Daniel was tongue-deep in her pussy, her eyes were on Marcus. His heart hiccupped at that small act. She met his eyes before dragging her gaze down his body until she looked at the growing hard-on tenting his jeans, and licked her lips.

Walking to her, he unbuttoned his jeans and pulled out his cock. Marcus ran his hand up and down his heavy dick.

"Do you want this, baby?" he asked as his jeans fell to his ankles and he stepped out of them. "Yeah, you want this, don't you? Right between those plump pink lips." His moved in closer, his hard-on a millimeter from her mouth, which was open and waiting to be filled.

"Who do you belong to, Carrie?" His heart was thundering in his chest as he waited for her answer. Instead of the words he needed to hear, she squealed and raised her hips off the bench.

Goddamn, Daniel, Marcus thought, shooting his best friend a dirty look. Daniel cocked his eyebrows and purposely drew long on Carrie's clit, causing her to moan even louder. The man was totally fucking with him, and he wasn't in the mood for it. If Carrie was going to moan, it would be with her lips wrapped around his cock.

He turned his attention back to Carrie. "Come on, baby, who do you belong to? Tell me what I want to hear and I'll give you a treat."

He dragged the head of his cock over her bottom lip, smearing the velvety surface with his pre-come before pulling back, out of reach.

"You, Marcus." Her voice a mere whisper.

"Louder. I can't hear you," he growled.

"Dammit, Marcus, you. I belong to you," she cried.

Marcus smiled and let his cock slip into her wet mouth. She sucked him hard into her. He hissed as a slight pain mixed with a hell of a lot of pleasure slid up his body. Little vixen. She'd used her teeth to scrape him underneath as she sucked hard on his head.

He reached down and pinched her nipple. "You'll pay for that later, baby," he promised. Then he went up in flames because instead of looking scared, her eyes became hazy and filled with even more lust at the thought of him punishing her.

Chapter Eleven

೧

Daniel wanted to give himself a pat on the back at the resentful looks Marcus kept sending him. His mission was accomplished. Marcus was good and pissed and incredibly territorial. Daniel knew it was a shitty thing to do but some people needed a friendly shove off the cliff before they got it. Marcus was one of those people. His best friend wasn't meant to be single forever, randomly fucking this woman or that one.

During many inebriated conversations when Marcus had let his famous guard down, he confessed that his swinging lifestyle wasn't satisfying. He accomplished all he needed in his work, had every luxury he could possibly desire and commanded attention wherever he went. But it wasn't enough anymore.

While he never came out and told Daniel directly that he wanted a woman to love him, it was there between the lines.

So when Carrie approached him about trying out the club, Daniel remembered the way Marcus looked at his sweet little assistant and a nutty idea had formed in his head.

He knew that "happily ever after" wasn't in the future for him, but Marcus was another matter entirely. Marcus wanted to be loved even if he wouldn't admit it, and Carrie clearly wanted to love him. What else could Daniel do but give them a gentle shove in the right direction? Hell, it was his responsibility as a friend!

Gazing up the length of Carrie's body, he grinned at the look of utter absorption on Marcus' face. Then he watched the way she was sucking Marcus off and it was the only proof Daniel needed. Yep, Marcus was hooked, hooked in a way that he never had been before, even with The Viper. If only he would admit it to himself.

Not that he blamed Marcus. Carrie tasted like fresh honey on his tongue. Sugary and sweet just like her personality. He drove his tongue in deeper, pulling her creamy goodness into his mouth. He lapped at her hot, tight little clit, loving the way she jumped whenever he bit down on it.

Fuck, he wished at times he could bed a woman this real, this sweet. One who wanted him like Carrie so obviously wanted Marcus. That was not to be his journey though, so he decided to enjoy tonight, because he was certain it would be the first, last and only time he'd ever be buried between the legs of a woman like this.

Marcus watched Carrie struggle to hold her orgasm in. She'd make a shitty poker player. Her brow was sweating, her body undulating from head to toe.

More than one of their previous lovers had claimed Daniel had a tongue that could drive a woman over the edge into madness. Marcus knew he would bring Carrie over and over to the brink, only to pull back until she calmed down. He could go on for hours like that. Marcus could not. He needed to be buried in Carrie. In the most intimate of kisses, skin to skin, he was going to have her.

Abruptly he stepped back from her. He was shaking as he untied her wrists, stroking the red marks left by the cuffs. Daniel stopped eating his *dessert* and helped Marcus guide Carrie from the bench and onto the bed.

"Assume your position." His voice was guttural with desire, nearly unrecognizable. As Carrie perched on spread knees, Marcus wondered if he'd ever tire of seeing her present herself to him. He decided he probably wouldn't.

He crawled after her, kneeling behind her on the bed. After tugging down his leathers, Daniel crawled to kneel in front of her.

Carrie instinctively sank back, melting into Marcus' body. He swallowed hard at the gesture. Carrie gave Daniel nothing more than brief glances, her eyes always shooting back to Marcus. While he'd known he needed that from her, he hadn't realized how much until he'd burned under the heat in her gaze.

It was humbling, this experience and this night with her. He knew his decision to bring Daniel into their bed was the right one. He had the answer to his silent question. The one he'd never have been able to ask Carrie directly.

It had been humiliating to find his wife going after Daniel. He'd never blamed his best friend; Daniel Ellis was utterly irresistible to women. But he'd also never been able to trust that any woman he kept in his bed for more than one night wouldn't turn to Daniel, too. Hell, Carrie herself had gone to Daniel to help her get into the club.

Here in his house, in his playroom, she gave Daniel little thought. Marcus felt like Tarzan. He wanted to beat on his chest and let out a howl of victory. Then he caught Daniel's eyes looking at him with what he swore was envy and he felt like a total shit.

Daniel knew, knew the reason Marcus had invited him here tonight. His friend had all but told him but seeing it was a different thing entirely. Fuck, Daniel deserved better than this. Marcus knew he was an asshole, he freely admitted it, but making his best friend feel like nothing more than a breathing sex toy was too much for even him.

Daniel had been there for him through his father's death, his divorce and subsequent humiliation. He'd even taken care of Meri when Marcus hadn't been able to do it himself. He needed to give his friend something but he knew he couldn't give him Carrie's beautiful, vulnerable eyes.

"Carrie," he whispered in her ear. Wrapping his hands underneath her breasts, he cupped them lightly. "Baby, I want you to talk to Daniel when he touches you. Tell him what makes you feel good."

Marcus squeezed lightly around the clamps, and Carrie moaned in response to the sharp bite of pain twining with dark pleasure as Marcus licked along her neck. "Kiss him for me, Carrie. I want you to make him come hard."

Daniel dipped his mouth to Carrie's, running his tongue over the velvety surface of her lips. She let her mouth melt into his, sucking his tongue into the hot cavern until he groaned and drew back, lips red and glazed with the moisture of their kiss.

Daniel drew one gentle finger over her cheek before shifting to lie back on the bed. Placing his hands on her hips, he urged her to lift up before sliding his shoulders between her spread knees and drawing her dripping pussy down to his voracious mouth. Carrie gasped as he slid two thick fingers up her aching passage.

Carrie jerked in ecstatic reaction but kept her head back, eyes locked with Marcus. He continued to talk to her, whispering how beautiful she looked, how well her body responded to his every desire.

"Let him feel how tight your pussy is, baby. How hot and wet you are. Show him your passion and hold nothing back."

Daniel chose that moment to suck her clit into his mouth, drawing hard on the little bundle of nerves. Carrie arched into his mouth and remembering Marcus' command stuttered out, "God, Daniel, suck harder. Your tongue feels so good."

With every word, Daniel drew harder on her flesh, emitting little growls of excitement as he moved to slurp at the syrup flowing freely from her spasming pussy.

"That's good, baby, tell him all about it." Marcus' words breathed over her skin, sending a shower of goose bumps to prickle over her entire body. "But what can't you do, baby?"

"I can't come, Marcus," she gasped. "But..." Her voice became sharp with arousal. "God, Daniel your mouth. You're going to make me come. Please slow down," she begged, grinding helplessly against Daniel's relentless tongue. "Please, I can't come yet."

Carrie felt her body tighten. For the first time tonight she was scared. The sensations Daniel was drawing from her body confused her. She belonged to Marcus. It seemed wrong for another man to be able to pull this sort of reaction from her.

Marcus seemed to know, to understand. He ran one hand down her spine and whispered for her ears only, "Do this for me, baby. I want you to. I need you to."

Carrie groaned helplessly as Daniel moved his head back just enough to speak, the words vibrating against her sensitive pussy lips. "Don't worry. I won't draw blood."

She let out a choked laugh that quickly turned to a scream of painful pleasure as he caught her clit between sharp teeth.

Carrie sank back into Marcus' embrace. Her hands, still lifting her breasts, holding them out like a gift for Marcus, began to clench convulsively. Marcus reached down, taking her arms and drawing them up behind her, circling his neck. Then he replaced her hands on her breasts with his own, pinching lightly at the nipples, flicking at the dangling clamps and causing her to thrash in his arms and emit little screams of pleasure at the molten sensations.

Just when she thought she couldn't stand another second, stretched on a rack of pleasure between Marcus and Daniel, Daniel dropped his head down to the bed, breathing raggedly for a moment before sliding gracefully out from under her. He rose to his hands and knees, crouching in front of her like a giant jungle cat. Hands still planted on the bed, he stretched up to catch her lips with his own.

His lips tasted of his unique musk and her arousal. He tasted nothing like Marcus. He kissed differently as well. Marcus was impatient when he kissed her. She felt like she was being branded by Marcus. Daniel, on the other hand, made kissing an art form. He was all finesse and subtle slides of his tongue here, a scrape of teeth there. With Daniel it was all about making her feel aroused. And damn, she was definitely aroused by this man.

Marcus removed her hands from his neck, and Carrie grasped Daniel's shoulders and pulled him to her. His body pressed flush with hers, his hard planes and lines melting into her soft curves. His obvious erection pushed against her soft belly.

Two days ago, she would never have envisioned being strapped to a table with two men but these men made her feel like the sexiest woman in the world.

Two large fingers slid to her cleft. Daniel groaned as his fingers pushed their way into the wet opening and found her tight and waiting for him. He kissed her even deeper while he stroked her wet flesh, and Marcus continued his ministrations on her breasts and neck.

"Fuck, Carrie. Do you have any idea how hot you look with Daniel's fingers sliding into you?" The gritted words just added to the fire flooding her body. To emphasize his point, Marcus pushed his large cock against her, rubbing along the hot skin on her lower back. "She feels amazing, doesn't she? All creamy and hot."

Chapter Twelve

ॐ

"Damn, Marcus. You lucky son of a bitch, you know exactly how she feels," Daniel rasped, sinking his fingers back into her welcoming cunt. Carrie was indeed hot and soft, and her hungry little pussy sucked his fingers in. She squeezed the muscles around him and he groaned his appreciation, lunging forward to latch his mouth to her neck as he added a third finger, stretching her. He wanted her soaking wet, because he was going to ride her hard.

"Touch my cock, Carrie," he ground out between bites to her throat. He knew he was marking her and had to bite back a smile as he imagined Marcus' reaction to Daniel's marks on his woman. Then the time for thinking was over.

He moaned deeply when she grasped him by the root. She pulled her hand up, and wasn't too gentle about it. He pushed himself farther into her grasp. God, she knew just how much pressure he needed to stay on the edge.

Reaching down, she cupped his balls, and the heated caress grabbed Daniel. He went back to kissing her. The three of them rocked back and forth as both men enjoyed the ebb and flow of bare skin rubbing against bare skin. When her thumb rubbed directly underneath his cock head, Daniel's eyes rolled back. He was too close to coming, and he wanted it to be inside her waiting heat. He pulled back reluctantly. Grabbing one of the condoms that were strewn on the table, he whisked it on in record time.

He lay on his back, guiding Carrie over him and pushing open her thighs.

"Ride me. Do it now." Daniel knew his voice was harsh but he couldn't seem to find his usual smoothness. If Carrie was unusual for Marcus, she was doubly so for Daniel. Everything about her response, so innocent and genuine, sent the blood flooding to his dick. Hell, everything about her turned him on.

His cock jumped and her eyes widened. If he hadn't been so fucking turned on, Daniel would have smiled at the sight. Marcus released her and she crawled farther up Daniel's torso. He grabbed his cock, stroking once, twice, before guiding it to her entrance, positioning it just so. She was so juicy and ready to be fucked that he slid in easily in spite of his large size and her small opening.

"Awww, fuck," he gasped. His hips bucked uncontrollably up into her waiting sheath. "Don't push down. Stay exactly where you are." It was nearly impossible to keep his voice commanding as he raised his hips to slam into her. Not when she felt so damned good that she stripped his control away one slow wriggle at a time.

She inhaled and groaned at his invasion. His cock was thicker than average, and it blew his mind the way her vaginal walls clung to the swollen, throbbing flesh. He moved into her, pumping his hips up, and he grasped her waist to keep her poised on her knees. With every thrust, she rewarded him with a gasp of pleasure. For every gasp, he rewarded her with a flick of his thumb over her clit.

They went on like this for several minutes while Marcus caressed her lower back and ass, wrapping his hands around the soft, pink-flushed cheeks. Clenching his fingers into her generous curves, he eased his thumbs into her crack, opening her for his hungry eyes.

Reaching down, Marcus snagged the small tube of lube he'd tossed on the bed earlier. He drizzled a line down her crack, watching it shimmer on her pale skin in the dim light of the room. Her shiver made the oil catch the light even more, reflecting sparkles on her flesh, like she'd been sprinkled with fairy dust.

Dragging his thumbs through the slick path of lube, Marcus began stroking in time with Daniel's thrusts, working first one thumb and then the other a tiny fraction into her waiting star. It was more of a pulsing at first; just enough to make her moan and wriggle back against him a little bit. But soon, that wasn't enough for either of them.

"Carrie, I want you to lean forward, and stay on your knees. Grab Daniel's head, baby."

She immediately did as he instructed, and Daniel groaned as two very healthy tits swung in his face. Unable to resist, he let his tongue reach out and touch the tips of each clamped nipple, which were bright red and painfully aroused.

Carrie was panting for him, gasping with each of Daniel's thrusts, trying to maintain her position and still push back against Marcus' invading thumbs. It was a good thing, he thought with dark amusement, that she was a good multitasker.

Finally Marcus decided to show her some pity and speared one thumb deep into the dark, forbidden recesses of her body.

She arched back with a scream, inadvertently slamming down on Daniel's cock at the same time. Daniel grunted and clamped her to him, obviously trying to maintain his control. Marcus' thick thumb pressed against him through the tissue-thin barrier separating them, making Carrie's already tiny pussy almost unbearably tight.

Marcus waited impatiently, watching Daniel until his friend gave a brief nod, and then loosened his hold on Carrie's hips.

"Lift up now, baby," Marcus directed in a harsh whisper. "Spread your legs wide for me." He pulled his thumb out and reached for the lube again. "Don't move your hands from where they are."

He opened the cap, lubricating his first two fingers before sliding them into her well-prepared ass. Slowly, he worked the lube in, thick and deep. When her tissues began to relax, he scissored his fingers, stretching her. She shivered at his touch.

"I'm going to take you here, baby. Just like I told you earlier." Slowly, he continued to prepare the tight hole, pushing through the ring of muscles. He returned several more times until the lube was sliding down her thighs.

"Here, Marcus," Daniel grunted, tossing him a condom as he held Carrie poised above him, only the tip of his erection piercing her willing flesh. Marcus knew that if he didn't use the condom, Daniel would know for sure how Marcus felt about Carrie. He knew it but he didn't care. All he cared about was tunneling into her, skin to skin. No barriers between him and his woman, ever.

He tossed the condom back onto the dresser as he squeezed lube along the length of his dick. Daniel actually barked out a laugh at the action but quickly shut up at the death gaze Marcus gave him. While Daniel was his best friend, he was also a pain in the ass. Especially when he thought he was right about something. Fortunately for his health and well-being, he was also smart enough to know when to back off. Usually.

Marcus was, after all, a Worthington. And a pissed-off Worthington was hell on anyone who got in their way.

Marcus placed a hand on each of Carrie's cheeks, parting her to his view. He guided his cock to the closed-up flower.

"Carrie, my cock is bigger than your little plugs, so you need to listen to me."

She shook her head. Her body trembled a little, out of fear or anticipation. Marcus figured it was a little of both. He pushed his cock slowly against her opening. Her ass tightened, fighting the intrusion.

"I need you to relax, baby." Fuck, she had to relax because he had to be inside her now! "When I push in, you need to push your ass toward me."

He probed farther.

"Daniel, play with her clit," he said harshly as her tight muscles tried to refuse his entry.

The other man brought one finger to Carrie's pink little cherry. As soon as he rubbed it, her ass flew back toward Marcus, and the thick head of his cock finally popped through the ring of muscles housed there.

Once he'd breached the opening, it was much easier to forge his way inside. Inch by inch, he worked his way into her excruciatingly tight, blisteringly hot little asshole. Finally, when he was all the way in, he went still, waiting for Daniel to make his move.

Carrie wailed like a banshee as Daniel dug his enormous cock into her greatly tightened pussy. Marcus could feel the other man's cock dragging along the length of his own and could only imagine how amazing it must feel for Carrie to be so completely filled, stuffed with cock.

They were both still for a moment, allowing Carrie time to adjust to two cocks being buried balls-deep in her. Marcus gripped her hips, Daniel steadied her arms, and they began to move. It took only a few thrusts to establish the familiar rhythm. As Daniel slid in, Marcus slid out. Daniel was still licking her sensitive nipples while lightly teasing her clit, and with every movement, Carrie moaned her enjoyment to the ceiling.

Her soft moans became louder and louder.

"That's right, baby, let us know how good it is to have us inside of you." Marcus teased her neck, licked her spine. He felt like a wolf in heat, claiming her with his teeth, leaving his mark against her pale, pale skin.

"She's so fucking tight." Daniel's voice was strained with the effort to keep control. Hell, Marcus knew how he was feeling, since he was fighting for his own control.

Marcus helped Carrie straighten up on Daniel. The position had his cock sinking deeper into her tight, little hole. Daniel grunted at the increased pressure, his hips jerking hard against her sex. Marcus knew that his friend wouldn't last much longer. Fuck, neither would he. It was time to up the stakes.

"You want to come for me, baby?" He whispered the question against her cheek. He wrapped his arms around her, cupping her breasts, toying with the clamps as she writhed in his arms.

"God, yes. Please, I need to come."

"Then come, baby." Carrie's head turned toward him, her arm reaching around his neck, and pulled him forward. He sucked in his breath. Her eyes begged him for something but he didn't know what.

"What is it, baby? What do you need?"

She blinked slowly and a single tear traced its way down her cheek.

"Do you need us to stop, baby? Do you need to say the word?"

She pulled harder on his neck, shaking her head wildly. "No, don't stop. Come, Marcus. Come with me. I need you to come with me."

Marcus' lips crushed over hers in a quick, bruising kiss.

"Oh yeah, baby," he said. His thrusts became harder, faster. "I can do that." He felt Daniel arch under her, felt the beginning pulse of his friend's orgasm through the delicate skin separating them. Daniel's groans seemed to go on for hours before he stilled and pushed her upward into Marcus' pounding cock while Marcus blindly pumped into her.

Marcus' balls tightened painfully as the orgasm built there and fought its way out of his dick. He pinched Carrie's nipples, gasping against her cheek, "Now, Carrie!" And then words were impossible as she tipped her head back and cried out. His own voice joined hers, his hot come shot deeply into her contracting ass. She clenched around him, squeezing him impossibly harder, wringing another load from his body.

Marcus held Carrie tightly to him as she pushed her face into his neck. He felt Daniel taking the clamps off of her nipples. He held her breasts up, offering her tender nipples for his best friend to lick and kiss soothingly. Carrie's tears fell hot against his neck.

Carefully, both men removed themselves from her worn-out body. She collapsed on the sheets. Marcus lay down next to her, stroking her hair, slowly rubbing circles on her back.

Daniel discreetly moved to the bathroom, where he began running water to draw Carrie a bath.

Carrie shuddered in Marcus' arms, shedding tears for him, for this night. He hoped for the pleasure the two men had given her. The water was shut off and Daniel came out of the bathroom. He stepped to the bed but before he could even offer to carry her to the waiting tub, Marcus bared his teeth in a snarl that would have done any territorial wolf proud.

Daniel gave him a brief, sad smile and turned away from the bed. He dressed quietly and turned to leave. Marcus got up and went to his best friend. Daniel didn't meet his eyes until he'd reached the door.

Marcus grabbed his friend around the upper arm as he reached for the knob.

The other man looked him in the eye. "Don't fuck this up," he said in a subdued voice.

Marcus shook his head ruefully. "It would help if I knew what the fuck *this* is."

His friend laughed. "Oh, I think it's pretty clear, buddy. She owns you, heart, soul and cock."

Marcus grimaced a little at the truth of the statement. He met Daniel's eyes again and was startled at the emptiness there.

"Fuck, Daniel. I didn't mean to use you. I didn't have to…"

Daniel interrupted briskly, "Yeah, you did. You needed to know that she wanted only you." His eyes cleared and his smile was as polished and perfect as ever when he added, "You got your answer."

Daniel opened the door. Marcus knew the look in his friend's eyes. Daniel needed to escape, and he needed to find the nearest bar.

"Daniel, wait."

Both men turned slowly at Carrie's soft voice. Wrapped in a silk sheet, she approached them. She moved in front of Marcus, so close he could feel her body heat radiating along his entire front.

Shyly, she raised her big brown eyes to meet Daniel's. "Thank you. I don't know if I could have done this with anyone else."

Daniel shook his head slightly. "Baby, I should be thanking you." He glanced up at Marcus, and with an evil grin wrapped one large hand around Carrie's neck and pulled her to him. He crushed her mouth under his, kissing her for the last time, taking one last taste of the honey that was Carrie. When both of them were breathing raggedly and Marcus was emitting a low, vicious growl, Daniel released her and with one last, slow smile, walked out the door.

"Never again, Carrie."

She turned to face him, and Marcus gently pushed her back against the door.

"I will never share you again." He whispered the words almost to himself as he bent his head and kissed her with a slow exploration that rocked her to the core.

She loved this man even more today than she had yesterday. More than she had ever thought possible.

She knew that in the light of the coming morning, she would cling to the picture of Marcus and the look in his steely gaze as it wandered over her face. Possession seemed carved into every line of his features. His smoky eyes seemed to shout *mine*. She pushed back the knowledge that it was really just *mine for now,* determined to wring every bit of pleasure that she could out of the weekend.

Chapter Thirteen

ൟ

"Go get into the bath, Carrie-mine." He stood waiting for her to obey. She could have sworn he wanted to say something else but he gave his head a shake and the moment passed. She went into his luxurious bathroom, leaving Marcus in the playroom.

The marble tub was huge, easily able to fit three or four people. Carrie felt a knot in her stomach as she wondered if Marcus entertained more than one woman at a time here. It made sense that he would and she chastised herself for getting upset. She didn't have the right to be jealous. This was only one weekend. Marcus, while possessive, had given her no indication that he wanted something more from her. She needed to get girlish fantasies out of her mind and concentrate on the moment. She'd known the rules from the beginning. He'd demanded one weekend, nothing more. She prayed that he would be asking for more come Sunday night.

Slipping into the hot tub, Carrie let the warmth melt into her skin, loosening sore, stiff muscles. Her pussy was tender and swollen, as were her nipples. Her ass burned like fire. She gathered soapy water and let it trickle over her neck and back. She was deliciously sore from head to toe, well used and totally satisfied sexually for the first time in her life.

The bathroom door opened and Marcus entered. He knelt at the side of the tub, grabbing a thick sponge. He doused it with sweet-smelling body wash and began bathing her body. He worked slowly, starting at her aching feet, rising to the curve of her calf. Carrie leaned back and enjoyed the feeling of being taken care of.

She closed her eyes, intent on enjoying the sensations, but Marcus had other ideas.

"Keep those damn eyes open." He sounded thoroughly tired when he spoke. She noticed the dark circles under his gray gaze. She watched his hands glide up her thighs, her belly and chest. He was careful to go easy on her still-red nipples. He reached her neck, stroking the sponge over her shoulders until she was warm, clean and completely relaxed.

He dropped the sponge and started to rise. Carrie caught his forearm. He stooped and looked at where she was holding him.

"Join me," she invited gently. She watched his hesitation grow as his arm tensed.

"Marcus, we only have two days. Join me and relax. Just for a little while."

He eyed her a moment then turned his face away. Taking a deep breath, he turned back, stepping carefully into the tub behind her.

Carrie leaned into his chest. Marcus closed his eyes and enjoyed the quiet, the feel of her skin sliding against his. Not fucking or screaming out her pleasure, just resting together. It was such a simple act but one that Marcus had never experienced before. Karen had never shared this kind of intimacy with him. No woman had. He swallowed hard, myriad emotions battling to take hold of him at once. A man could get used to this.

He was so fucking torn and he didn't like the feeling. He was left weak and unsure of himself for the first time in his life.

Daniel. He'd never come so close to hurting someone physically as he had his best friend. The minute Daniel had laid his hands on Carrie, Marcus had felt as if he'd been sucker punched.

He idly ran his hands up and down her arms. Caressing soft skin, he inhaled her scent, which lingered in the air. He didn't think he'd ever get enough of it, of her.

His first instinct was to tuck Carrie in her car and send her home. Cut all ties and leave them both in one piece, but he wouldn't. He was still a selfish bastard and he didn't want this to end yet. Besides, a tiny voice whispered in his heart, it was already too late to avoid heartache.

Absently, his arms crept around, clasping in front of her, holding her close. His mouth lingered on his favorite spot on her body, the back of her neck.

He listened to her breathe, felt her heart beating against his chest. Fuck, why did he feel this way now? Goddamn it, this wasn't a complication he needed.

She suddenly turned from his embrace and slid to the opposite side of the tub, her gaze rising over his chest and back to his eyes. His arms felt empty, his entire body cold without her in his arms. He couldn't help himself. He had to ask the dreaded question.

"Are you okay?" He hadn't meant to sound harsh but it came out that way.

Carrie hiked her eyebrow and smiled.

"I'm fine." She gave that mysterious little smile that never failed to make him crazy. "I'm better than fine." Her smile widened. "In fact, I don't think I've ever been this good."

He didn't particularly care for the satisfied expression on her pretty little face. Was she thinking of him or Daniel, or that she'd been pleased by not one but two men? He grunted then realized how loud the sound had been when her eyes darkened and she licked her lips.

"Carrie, you racked up several punishments this evening. You don't listen very well." He wanted to laugh when the little vixen pouted her lips.

"I don't know what you mean," she argued, batting her eyelashes as she smiled coyly at him.

Marcus rubbed his hand over his mouth, hiding his smile at her teasing, then pointed to the place in front of him. "Present yourself to me, baby. Now."

Carrie slid across the tub, kneeling between his thighs. Placing her hands under her breasts, she lifted them and held them out for him to enjoy. He leaned forward and pulled one nipple into his mouth. He was playing rough with the peak, nibbling it, biting sharply then sucking until she gasped from the pleasure/pain.

He backed off and suckled gently when she whimpered, laving his tongue over her entire breast, applying the gentlest of touches until she was squirming, begging for more. He devoured her other breast in the same manner.

"You are so fucking hot, baby," he rasped against her red, throbbing nipple. "This would be so pretty with a little gold hoop." He flicked his tongue over one red peak. "If you wanted to please your Dom, you'd get two sexy little ruby hoops here."

It was a slipup, implying they had a future, but he didn't care. She only seemed to melt further the more he laid claim to her.

His cock was perilously close to her pussy and he could tell she was dying to be touched. Marcus smiled against her skin. Popping her nipple from his hungry mouth, he stood up, dragging his stiff length along her torso as he rose. He stepped from the tub and held out a hand.

Carrie wanted to scream in frustration. Her body was humming with unfulfilled longing. She couldn't believe how wet she was, even after the incredible sex she'd had less than an hour ago. But there she stood, taking Marcus' hand, wanting nothing more than for him to throw her to the floor and ride her hard.

Apparently he was having none of that. Instead he grabbed a big fluffy towel and began drying her off. It was an exercise in keeping as still as possible. When he finished with her, he tossed the towel in the corner.

"Now it's your turn, Carrie." When Carrie went to grab another towel, Marcus stopped her. "Not with a towel, baby."

"Then what would you like me to use," she asked, confused until his thumb slid over her bottom lip.

"Use your mouth. I want to feel that hot tongue sliding over every inch of me."

Her heart slammed into her throat. She hadn't gotten the chance to explore Marcus' body. Now she was going to know every part of it. She wanted Marcus to suffer as she was suffering. She wanted him to feel the heat rise and be helpless to do anything about it.

Carrie grinned. She felt truly devilish as she walked around his back. Kneeling, she placed her lips at his ankle. She slid slowly up his leg, licking every single drop of water from his hard muscles. She discovered a small scar along the back of one knee and flicked her tongue over it, smiling when the muscles clenched in response. The coarse hair lightly covering his legs tickled her nose as she continued a path up the back of his thighs.

She gently nudged his thighs and he widened his stance. Licking along the insides, she carefully nibbled his flesh here and there. He tried to hold in his pleasure but by the time her tongue and teeth rounded one tight ass cheek, Marcus no longer bothered to hold anything in. Instead he encouraged her.

"Mmmm, that's it baby," he hissed when her mouth danced a pattern between his ass cheeks and back down. He shuddered as her tongue touched him there over and over.

"*Fuck*, Carrie." His uncontrolled outburst only encouraged her more. She licked her way back up his ass, along the length of his spine, lapping tight skin and the strong sinew housed underneath. This was a powerful man; powerful in his body as well as his mind. Carrie's body was singing.

He watched her through stormy eyes as she moved to face him. Her tongue snaked along his jaw. She lapped at the droplets of water clinging to hot flesh.

She lowered her mouth to his flat male nipples, licking them gently before biting one hard enough to rock him on his feet. His erect cock hit Carrie's damp skin as she knelt again, this time in front of him.

She stroked the front and sides of his thighs. Her mouth watered at the sight of the single dewy drop hanging from the tip of his swollen head. Her eyes darted to his and she gasped at the expression she found there. His eyes were wild, molten. Inflamed herself, she leaned forward, running her tongue along his heavy sac.

She had only a second to prepare before he fell to his knees. Hands on her hips, he spun her around so she was facing away from him. Excitement sliced through her. She felt the silk belt from one of the robes hanging on the back door wrapping around her arms from elbow to wrist, binding them tightly in front of her.

He placed a folded up towel on the floor and guided her down until her forehead hit the towel.

"Carrie, you drive a sane man to madness," he groaned before filling her in one hard thrust.

Marcus leaned over her, trying to slow the force of his thrusts, not letting her see his face as he fucked her. He couldn't let her see his control give way to something so foreign, so terrifying that he'd been left with only two choices: run like hell or fuck her hard. Marcus didn't run. Instead he chose to sink himself into the one person who knew him better than anyone else in the world. The one person who scared him to death and the one person who deserved a hell of a lot more than Marcus could ever give.

"Please." Her cry drew him out of thought as she pushed against him.

He grabbed her hair, pulling slightly, lifting her head up. "Please what, Carrie?"

"Please, Marcus. I need you to fuck me harder. I need to come."

He needed no more encouragement. Pulling back until only the very crown of his cock lodged inside her, he made a sudden thrust forward, slamming into her welcoming heat. His thumb pressed against the delicate hole in her ass. She cried out for more and began to move in concert with him.

"That's it, ease back into me," he whispered, desperate to feel her wrapping those creamy walls tight around him. "Feel me, baby. Feel me taking you hard and deep. Like no one else."

Carrie was mewling and wiggling. His thumb delved a little deeper into her ass.

"Tell me, Carrie-mine, have you ever been taken like this? So fully? Have you ever given a man everything?" He was playing with fire, asking for something he wasn't able to give in return, but in this moment Marcus didn't give a fuck. He wanted her answer. He tugged her hair.

"Answer me, baby. Tell me." It was as close to begging as Marcus had ever come to in his life.

"No, no man has ever taken me this way." She was shaking. "I've never given another soul what I've given you."

He knew that later her confession would make him uneasy but for now Marcus only felt the triumph of having his woman beneath him, offering him everything, totally at his mercy.

He balls tightened and lifted, he quickly slid a finger against her clit and rubbed. Her head rolled back as she moaned in earnest. It was more than Marcus could take.

"Come, Carrie," he bellowed as his orgasm shot hard into her welcoming depths. He pumped over and over until his cock jerked from the sensitivity of sliding into her recesses.

He stayed crouched over her for a long time, savoring her heat, the snug clasp of her twitching pussy on his softening cock. Finally, reluctantly, he pulled out.

With shaky hands, he grabbed a wet washcloth, washing himself off then stroking the cloth over her thighs but avoiding her pussy, unwilling to wipe away all the traces of his possession from her body. He liked knowing his seed marked her as his. With her hands still tied, he helped her rise to her knees, and then to stand.

Wrapping his arm around her, he held her tightly. They walked slowly out of the bathroom, through the playroom and down the hall into his bedroom. The significance of her being the first female in his room since his divorce—the only woman to sleep with him in this house—wasn't lost on Marcus. He helped her to perch on the side of the bed. Pushing her thighs apart, Marcus knelt between her legs.

He untied her arms, rubbing the angry red marks left by the belt, kissing them again and again. When he finally looked up, his breath caught in his throat. Carrie showed no fear over the hard way he'd taken her. Instead her eyes were filled with fire, an obvious desire for more. He leaned forward, pressing a kiss to her forehead.

"You did well tonight." The compliment brought a small smile to her face. Damn, he loved that smile. Marcus stood and pulled the covers back. "Lie down, baby. You need your rest."

She snuggled down as he tucked the comforter over her body.

"Aren't you coming to bed?" Her voice was already sleepy, her eyes utterly sated.

"In a bit. I have some business I need to check on first." He bent down, kissing the frown from her face then, turning, he left the room, not daring to look back.

He needed to get out of here and regroup, because if he went back and got into bed with her, he would never let her leave it again.

Marcus decided it was time to step back, at least until he could get himself under control.

Chapter Fourteen

ଏ

The tantalizing aroma of coffee filtered into Carrie's dream, tempting her from sleep. She opened her eyes, blinking against the bright sunshine sifting through the curtains. Marcus lay on his side next to her holding a cup of liquid bliss.

"Good morning, baby. Or maybe I should say good afternoon." His smile lit his face.

"What time is it?" she asked, pushing up on one elbow and reaching greedily for the coffee, certain that it couldn't be *that* late.

"Almost one," he replied, pressing the cup into her hand.

She lifted the cup to her face, breathed in the heavenly steam and took a sip. Damn, she really needed the caffeine.

Marcus took the coffee from her and she sat up against the pillows at her back. He took a tray filled with food off the nightstand.

Carrie scanned the contents of the tray; it was piled high with fruit, croissants and butter. Decorative jars held jam and honey, and a crystal decanter held orange juice. Her stomach growled and when she covered it up, trying to stop the offending noise, Marcus laughed.

"It's all right. You worked up one hell of an appetite last night."

He picked up a strawberry and brought it to her lips. She scrunched up her nose at the plump piece of fruit.

"Don't like strawberries?" Marcus asked, popping the berry into his mouth.

Carrie shook her head. "Love them. They don't like me. I'm allergic. If I eat one, you'll have to take me to the hospital for a shot or else I'll swell up so bad my face will disappear."

Marcus picked up a slice of banana. "I assume these are okay?"

"Yes, I'm only allergic to the strawberries. And ragweed," she added.

He lifted the fruit to her lips. She allowed him to slide the slice of banana into her mouth, savoring the feeling of his finger along her tongue.

"You're lucky you have no allergies," she continued after she'd swallowed the sweet morsel. "Heck, I can't even go out into the sun without a gallon of sunscreen or I turn as red as a lobster."

Marcus fed her some more fruit: grapes, banana and orange slices. "You know a lot about me but apparently I don't really know anything about you."

Carrie just shrugged, a bit embarrassed that she'd shared some very intimate moments with a man who knew practically zero about her outside of the office.

Marcus stood. "It seems like I have some catching up to do."

He walked over to his closet and pulled out a garment bag along with a shopping bag.

"I got something for you to wear today. Why don't you take a shower and meet me downstairs."

He took the tray away, kissing her lightly on the nose. When he shut the door to his room, Carrie shuffled out of bed. Stretching her arms high above her head, she savored the well-worked feeling of all her muscles. Her body still held a tinge of soreness but she was thrilled by the small amount of pain. It reminded her in vivid detail of last night.

Taking one last sip of coffee, she turned curiously to the bags Marcus had laid across the bed. Since she would be leaving tomorrow, she planned to enjoy the day. Tomorrow was soon enough to think about when they would part ways. On Sunday, she could worry about having to start her new life without him. In the meantime, she planned to spend the next two days showing him exactly how much he needed her in his life.

She shook her head. Banishing the thoughts, she grabbed the clothes Marcus had set out for her and headed for the shower.

Marcus sat at the table, reading the paper, occasionally looking at his laptop. No urgent messages from Meri, so everything at work was well under control. Not that he had any worries where his little sister was concerned. She was more than capable of running the whole damn company if she wanted to.

There were many times when he dreamed of walking away from the responsibilities that he'd been tied to since his birth. The eldest Worthington, Stirling's protégé, he was more like his father than he wanted to admit. The older Marcus got, the more he realized he didn't want to live in the shadow of the Old Man. He sure as hell didn't want to die the way Stirling had, on a cold marble floor, disappointed in his children and cursing their existence. He only wished he'd been witness to the cruelty Meredith was subjected to.

If he'd known, he would have taken her from that house. The guilt gnawed at him even five years later. He could never make up to her for all the wrongs that she'd suffered. But in true Worthington fashion, Meri put on a stoic face and went on with her life.

Marcus' depressing musings were interrupted by Carrie's entrance into the dining room. He put the paper down and pointed to his lap.

She laughed. "I think that chair is a little too delicate to hold us both."

His arm shot out, grabbing her around the waist. She yelped as he pulled her into his lap.

"Baby, you don't worry about that," he said, kissing her neck and inhaling her scent. Ah, vanilla. He wanted to eat her up.

His body began to heat up. He savored his response but he had no intention of acting on it just yet. This afternoon was dedicated to relaxing and talking. He'd realized how little he knew about his woman, and he was determined to remedy the situation. He wanted to know everything there was to know about Carrie Anderson.

Last night as he'd sat nursing a warm beer and reliving every moment they'd ever spent together, he'd come to a conclusion that surprised him. He didn't want their time together to end on Sunday.

While the idea terrified him, something stronger was driving him. A sense of rightness, a sense of peace. Hell, a sense of being truly home for the first time in his life.

He was comfortable with Carrie. He enjoyed her smile, her intelligence and her looks of surprise when he demanded something from her. And he just plain loved watching those whiskey-brown eyes grow dark with arousal.

He was pleased to see her wearing the outfit he'd bought her. It was a simple sheath dress that flowed gently over her curves, ending just above the knee. The red floral pattern looked amazing against her creamy skin and showed off her velvet collar perfectly. A pair of flat sandals perfect for walking completed the outfit. She'd confined her silky, dark hair in a high ponytail. That just wasn't going to cut it.

"You look beautiful, except for this," he said, pulling the scrunchie out of her hair. He finger-combed the long, soft tresses around her face. "I love your hair down. Besides," he kissed the back of her neck, "I couldn't keep my hands or mouth to myself with that tender flesh tempting me all day." He paused to nibble behind her ear. "Okay, let's go."

"Where are we going?" Carrie asked, her excitement clearly written on her face. She didn't hide her emotions and Marcus liked that. He'd noticed the troubled expression on her face every time she was reminded that they only had this weekend together. Did she really want more than that? It was something to think about, but not now. Now it was time to take her out on a sunny afternoon and just spend time with her.

* * * * *

Carrie was having the time of her life. Marcus drove them to the small town of Royal Oak, a local community popular for its art galleries and sidewalk cafes. He parked at one end of town and they walked down the streets, going into the small shops that lined the way. She wasn't familiar with the area and was fascinated by all the unique things she discovered.

In a used bookstore, she came across an old romance she'd read in her late teens. The Valerie Sherwood novel featured a pirate and a scantily clad and very beautiful damsel embracing provocatively on the cover. Marcus teased her to no end about her choice in reading material but she didn't mind and allowed him to purchase the old book for her.

They stopped at a small gallery that featured independent local artists. None of the artists were well-known but the talent displayed was amazing. She was enthralled with the works mounted to the white walls.

A small painting held her attention the longest. It was a picture of lovers embracing. The artist had focused in on their entwined arms. The sepia tones added a sense of intimacy to the image that held her attention. She peeked at the discreet price tag hanging next to the piece and stifled her disappointment. Five hundred dollars was a little too steep for her budget. She stepped away and wandered around some more.

She felt him behind her. "You enjoyed that painting, didn't you?"

"Yes, I did." She grabbed his hand. "It was simple but there was just something so powerful about it. It made me feel like I was seeing something so intimate." She shook her head. "I don't know how to explain it."

He pulled her into his arms. "It's yours if you want it."

Her smile turned to a frown. "Marcus, a two-dollar used book is one thing but I couldn't allow you to buy me such an extravagant gift. Really, but thank you."

"If it pleases you, I want you to have it."

She cut him off by placing her mouth over his. The last thing she needed was a picture to remind her of their time together. Besides, Carrie never wanted Marcus to think she was after him for his money. The clothes he gave were different. It was a way for him to control her, and he gave her no real choice. A gift like this was entirely different.

She pulled his hand, tugging him out of the gallery. "Come on, big spender. I want to check out the shops across the street."

Marcus followed her, squeezing her hand. He glanced back at the small gallery. She'd turned down his offer. He was surprised, oddly, pleasantly so. Karen would have bought half the gallery and not even glanced at the small but powerful picture that caught Carrie's eye.

The picture was so simple yet full of passion. Just like Carrie herself. Marcus wanted to go back and buy the painting for her but decided against it. He would honor her wishes for now.

The afternoon flew by. Carrie's excitement over the smallest details had Marcus seeing things through her eyes. She was enchanted by the simplest things, like that damn ratty book she insisted on getting. He could imagine her on a rainy day, all curled up on the sofa with her novel.

He liked being with her. He'd always enjoyed her company at work—now he found that he liked her just as much outside of the office. She was fun, easy to be with. Easy to talk to. It was so nice to fully relax and not have to fucking worry about everything he said or did.

He couldn't seem to keep his hands off of her. He found himself touching her constantly, holding her, stroking her arm or just guiding her with a hand on the small of her back.

"Are you hungry?" he asked, brushing his lips across her temple.

"Mmmm, famished," she replied as he wrapped his arms around her, holding her tightly to him.

"Let's get something to eat then head back home. *I'm* hungry for you, woman," he whispered into her ear.

She laughed, stepping from his hold. "Then let's eat fast." She grinned and grabbed his hand, swinging their linked hands between them. "Lead the way."

Chapter Fifteen

ຂ໐

Marcus chose a small café with a patio surrounded by intricate black iron-work. He'd also chosen their menu — crisp salads draped in exotic cheeses and Mediterranean vegetables. The food was amazing, and nothing Carrie would have chosen for herself. Her weekend with Marcus was broadening her horizons in more ways than one.

They talked through the entire meal. She shared funny stories of the wicked escapades she and her sister had carried out, much to their parents' dismay. She kept Marcus in stitches with her description of her mother's reaction to the "designer haircut" she'd given Cassidy when she was ten and Cass was eight. Even better was the look on her father's face when, at sixteen and fourteen, the sisters bleached their hair out before dying it purple and blue.

Marcus reciprocated, sharing stories about life as a young Worthington that made her thank God for her parents. He had no hijinks to share; old Stirling wouldn't have tolerated them. His stories let her understand his need for control on a whole new level and she was touched and grateful that he trusted her enough to share them.

As the waiter cleared the table, he caught her sending a wistful glance at the dessert tray. There was a chocolate éclair calling her name but she just couldn't justify the calories.

Without a pause, he ordered the luscious dessert, prompting her to protest.

"Marcus, I appreciate that you like my curves but I'd rather not add any more to them!"

He merely shook his head and replied, "Baby, you don't ever need to worry about your curves when you're with me.

We'll definitely find a way to work the calories off." When she still looked unconvinced, he conceded. "Okay, how about we share it?"

Realizing that this was a battle she couldn't win, Carrie decided to give in gracefully. That was easy to do when the dessert arrived and he offered her the first heavenly bite.

She'd closed her eyes to savor the taste, so she was caught completely off guard by the caustic female voice that seemed to rip through their serenity like a rusty knife.

"Oh, look darling. My ex-husband is sharing a cream puff with a cream puff!"

Carrie didn't bother to look behind her. She knew what she'd find. Instead she locked her gaze on Marcus, who'd gone rigid with The Viper's first word. She could see the storm brewing in his eyes and she gently placed her hand over his, hoping to avoid the blowup she sensed coming.

Obviously not satisfied with their lack of reaction, Marcus' ex-wife moved to the side of the table. With her was a tall, dark-haired man. Carrie supposed he was attractive enough, in a *Godfather*, mercenary sort of way, but his oiled hair and dead eyes made her distinctly uncomfortable.

The Viper hadn't changed much. Still beautiful, still blonde, still runway tall and thin, she still embodied everything Marcus tended to look for in a date. She was lovely to look at but the lines around her eyes and mouth weren't signs of laughter. They were the outward marks of the bitterness that seeped from her very pores.

"Oh," she continued in an ingenuous voice, "it just gets better!" She slapped playfully at her companion's arm. "It's his *secretary!*"

"You sound surprised, love." The man with The Viper had a voice as smooth and oily as his hair. "Obviously your former husband can't keep a good woman." He paused and lifted Karen's thin, bony hand to his lips. "So he must turn to the common folk."

Karen gave Carrie a malicious smile. "Indeed you're right, Carlo. A pudgy little thing like this," she gestured contemptuously toward her, "is all he could find to play his nasty little games."

Marcus was all but vibrating now with rage, and frankly Carrie wasn't far behind him. Still, she was determined to hold her tongue. Anything she said would just encourage the woman. And Marcus didn't seem to have a problem with her appearance or job status, so she didn't feel any burning need to defend herself. But when The Viper attacked Marcus, that was another thing entirely.

Karen's light laugh faded and apprehension replaced the glee in her icy blue eyes as Marcus scowled wrathfully. Before he could speak, though, Carrie beat him to the punch, standing to face The Viper and her greasy companion.

"Karen."

The other woman flicked her eyebrow at Carrie's familiarity. While she'd been married to Marcus, she'd always been Mrs. Worthington.

"I realize that someone of your intellect would have such...*base* amusements but I really must ask you to leave our table."

The other woman looked dumbfounded but Carrie wasn't done.

"I would have thought Marcus made his distaste for your presence quite clear when he divorced your bony, silicone-filled ass, but perhaps the message wasn't clear enough."

Karen now wore an expression of narrow outrage. Her male friend looked amused until she shot a glance in his direction. Then he adopted a suitably fierce scowl.

"Marcus doesn't want you." There was a rush of satisfaction in saying the words. The ugly red flush that washed over The Viper's face was just icing on the cake. "And, since he can have pretty much anyone he *does* want, I'm happy that he wants me."

Karen looked ready to attack. Carlo looked like he was imagining what exactly Marcus saw in Carrie. Marcus looked ready to commit murder.

"Now, run along with your new friend and leave us alone." Having spoken her mind, she sat down and waited for the fireworks to start. It didn't take long.

"Are you going to let that little slut speak to me that way?" Karen's shriek had their fellow diners looking up in interest. Carlo shook his head and tried to guide Karen from the table, still casting speculative looks in Carrie's direction. Karen wouldn't be budged.

"Marcus Worthington, you make her apologize right now and maybe I won't see your entire family and that mausoleum of a company splashed across the front page of the *Free Press*!" Her long red nails were claws as she strained against Carlo, all her focus narrowed on Marcus. "You think you've seen the worst I can do." Her red lips moved in a snarl, her beauty distorted by her rage. "You've seen nothing, darling. Absolutely nothing."

Carrie didn't like the ugly turn the encounter was taking and she didn't want to see it escalate. In a desperate move to distract him, she rose and slipped around the table, sliding onto Marcus' lap as if she'd been born to be there.

He was still shaking with rage but as she wrapped her arm around his back, squeezing tightly, she felt him begin to calm. Slightly. When he finally spoke, his voice was icy but he seemed under control.

"Karen, we are no longer married." His eyes were glacial as they raked disparagingly over her. "You don't get to comment on my friends, my lovers, my company or my life. Today you've managed to insult all of them."

Carrie tunneled her free hand through his thick hair when his voice began to rise, once again drawing the attention of their fellow diners.

"I left you, and you made it clear you wanted nothing more to do with me, either." Karen's eyes were narrowed slits of malice as Marcus spoke dismissively to her. "Keep it that way. Go play with your new toy and leave me and my woman alone."

With that, Marcus very obviously turned his attention to Carrie, scooping up a bit of cream filling from their melting dessert with one finger and offering it to her.

Pretending the malevolent couple wasn't there, she daintily licked his finger clean before sucking it into the warm cavern of her mouth. There wasn't really anything sexual in the move. It was more about ownership. Marcus claimed her and now she was claiming him.

"You'll regret this, Marcus Worthington." Karen's voice was a vicious hiss, like the viper Daniel had named her for. "Just wait and see. One of these days, your charmed existence will collapse around your perverted ears." Marcus continued to ignore her, so Carrie did likewise. "We'll see who's laughing then!"

Carlo finally succeeded in dragging Karen away and Carrie let herself wilt in Marcus' lap.

"Wow," she commented softly. "You were married to that." When Marcus growled again, she stroked his cheek. "I'm just amazed that you divorced her instead of stabbing her to death with a butter knife."

His growl turned into a choked laugh and he finally relaxed, burying his face against her neck.

Chapter Sixteen

ɛɔ

Marcus was brooding. He knew it but couldn't seem to stop. Carrie had coaxed him into finishing their dessert but they'd never regained the easy camaraderie of earlier. Each bite had been like ashes in his mouth. All he could taste was the bitter memory of his ex-wife's betrayal.

They'd fallen silent by the time they reached the car. Marcus ushered her in but when she tried to engage him in conversation, rather than answer her he opted to turn the radio up loud to one of the classic rock stations.

His knuckles were white against the steering wheel, and the lack of control just pissed him off more. Taking a deep breath, he concentrated on controlling his breathing, his muscles and his mind. Karen had emasculated him once, he'd be damned if he'd let her do it again.

No, he was a Dom. That had been at the basis of their problems. He cast a look in Carrie's direction. Carrie claimed that was what she wanted in her bed. A Dom. He still didn't think she knew what she was asking for.

She was already so much more important to him than Karen had ever been. Marcus refused to put a name to his feelings but he suspected he wouldn't survive a betrayal like Karen's if it came from Carrie.

He had to know. Before he destroyed them both, he had to know if Carrie really wanted his lifestyle. If she could handle it. If she could handle him.

They might not have any future beyond tomorrow but he knew that they definitely had no future if Carrie couldn't take all he had to give her.

As they drove back to Marcus' house, Carrie could feel his agitation growing and wished there was something she could do or say to make things all right for him again. Finally she decided not to say anything. Marcus' feelings about his divorce and The Viper were something he needed to work out. And he needed to do it on his own.

Just as her anxiety began to mirror his, they pulled into his driveway.

It was early evening and the house was dark when he ushered her inside. Marcus led her straight to the playroom, still silent as he closed the door behind them.

He looked at her for a brief moment. When she opened her mouth to ask him if he was okay, Marcus placed a finger on her lips.

"Not a word. You may beg, moan, even scream." He stroked his finger down her chin, tracing the line of her throat. "But otherwise, you may not speak." His voice took on that deep, gravelly quality she'd only heard when he was truly pissed and wanted no argument. She'd heard him use that tone of voice on people when a project wasn't going in the right direction. It signaled the presence of the dangerous and dark Marcus. The one who frightened the strongest of men.

"Strip," he commanded, still in that frightening tone. She obeyed without hesitation. He might be angry but she knew his anger was not directed at her, and she trusted him absolutely.

He stepped behind her, ghosting his hands down her arms as her dress slid to the floor. When she stood in nothing but her black lace bra and panties, he reached around to grab ahold of both breasts. His fingers pulled and flicked at the buds of her nipples and she could feel his ragged breath on her neck as he watched them harden.

She laid her head back against his shoulder. His breath was heavy in her ear. She shivered as his tongue snaked out and licked the shell of her ear before biting down on the lobe.

Marcus loved nipping and biting and she loved for him to do it. Her entire body bore the reminders of where his teeth and lips had sucked at delicate, pale flesh. She loved every dark purple spot she carried. They came from the man she loved, the man she would have to leave tomorrow.

Suddenly sad, forlorn feelings enveloped her. She closed her eyes as Marcus increased the pressure on her breasts. This was *not* the time to be thinking of life without him. She had one more night and the day tomorrow; there was no point in rushing the sadness that she would soon experience when she walked through the door of his house for the last time.

Marcus unhooked her bra and pulled off her panties, leaving her naked in front of him. He led her to the platform in the center of the room. Still holding her hand, he helped her step onto the highest riser.

"Arms up," he instructed.

Carrie complied. He quickly fastened two soft leather cuffs around her wrists and attached a long rope. He pulled the rope upward. She followed the motion with her eyes and discovered that the rope was threaded through a sturdy hook in the ceiling. After securing the rope, he repeated the process with her legs, securing her ankles to the far edges of the platform. The position stretched her almost to her toes and kept her arms high above her head.

He left the room without a word, and Carrie looked around the large space. She was already wet with anticipation of what he was going to do to her.

Her nipples were so hard, her pussy so soft. She needed him inside of her. He could take her right now with no preliminaries. She was that ready for him.

When he returned, he'd shed his shirt and shoes. He stood barefoot and bare-chested, his black jeans hanging low on his hips. He carried a glass filled with clear liquid and ice, and a black silk bag.

He stood facing her and raised the glass to his lips. After taking a small sip, he reached out his chilled tongue and drew it up the vulnerable line of her throat. When she sucked in a breath, he took the glass and slid it up the curve of her breast before tilting it to drizzle a tiny, icy stream toward her nipple. The cold shocked her and she hissed as the liquid slid down her breast, followed by his now-hot tongue.

Marcus bent forward and licked the liquid from her body, savoring his drink. He repeated the move over and over until she thought she'd go mad, until she was literally pushing her hips forward with the need to be filled.

"So impatient," Marcus rumbled. "Maybe this will help." He reached into the bag and pulled out the largest dildo Carrie had ever seen.

Her eyes popped wide and her thighs tried to close at the sight of the monster. "Marcus, there is no way that will fit."

He only grinned as he pulled out a bottle of lube. He kept his eyes on hers as he dripped a line of the slippery stuff down one side of the dildo. Carrie knew she must look nervous, because his grin quickly faded and he growled, "You only have to say the word, baby, and we'll stop."

She didn't like the finality in his words. He brought the toy up to her breasts, rubbing it lightly across each lush globe.

"If you haven't learned to trust that I know what you can and can't take, say the word, baby."

He pressed the head of the toy to her lips. She stared into stormy gray eyes for a moment. Did she really trust him that much? *Stupid question*, she thought. Absolutely, she did. She trusted Marcus with her very life.

Opening her lips, she licked the large head. Marcus seemed to exhale slightly at her acceptance.

One big hand slid between her thighs, and he groaned. "Damn, you are so fucking wet already."

His fingers dipped inside of her, making shallow thrusts. Carrie moved her hips forward, trying to lure his pumping fingers deeper, but he would have none of that. He just continued his short, shallow strokes, occasionally spicing things up by sweeping his thumb over her clit.

She whimpered and writhed under the whip of sensation, and he chuckled darkly. Just when she thought she couldn't hold on, she was going to come, he pulled out. Leaning back, he ran the dildo down the front of her chest, sliding across her tummy and touching her lower lips. He teased her opening with it.

"Make those thighs wide for me. Baby, I'm going to fill you up."

Carrie widened her stance as much as the ropes would allow. The toy tickled the sensitive nerves at her entrance. Marcus reached down, spreading more of the cool, slick lube around her entrance. She cried out as he began rubbing her clit.

He'd taken an ice cube and was moving it back and forth along her clit at the same time as he worked the toy into her resisting body. One slow inch at a time. It stretched Carrie so fully she thought it would tear her in two. She felt her body fall into a vortex of confusion, not knowing what sensation to focus on. The icy caress of his fingers? The heavy invasion of the dildo?

Just as she was about to beg him to stop, he pulled the toy out. Before she could draw a breath of relief, he slid it back in, setting up a rhythm that soon had her moaning. The pain quickly bled into a dark pleasure. Each time he stretched her to the limit, she found that she wanted more.

The ice cube had melted and was replaced by his chilly fingers; they warmed quickly against her hot, pulsating cunt.

She was fast approaching the edge, her orgasm rising quickly.

"Marcus, I'm going to come."

He never paused in his motions, never even looked up from her pulsing pussy. All he did was grit out, "Oh no, you aren't."

Even as the words came out of his mouth, she lost the battle against her orgasm, tossing her head back and shuddering in her bonds. Before she'd even begun to come down, the toy was pulled out. She whimpered at the empty feeling.

Marcus pushed his hands through the back of her hair, pulling her head back.

"How many times do I have to tell you, Carrie, that you don't come until I tell you to?" His eyes were bleak and he sounded so disappointed that she wanted to cry.

"Marcus, please," she managed to sob.

He let go of her hair, palming her cheek. "You don't trust me at all, baby. What a pity," was all he said.

He walked away, leaving her shaking in her bonds, confused and upset. Just when she was sure he would leave the room entirely, he stopped and retrieved the black bag. Sending her a dark glance, he pulled out another toy, this one a vibrator. Looking at her from under his brows, he stalked around her before settling on his knees at her feet and sliding the vibrator in, in, in to her still-pulsing pussy. Holding her gaze with his own, he cranked the speed up until her body was shaking with the need to spill itself again.

When he had her shaking and crying, he moved behind her. She was startled when her arms dropped by several inches. When he'd given her a foot or so of slack, he commanded, "Lean forward."

She folded her upper body as far over as she could and felt the cords secured so she couldn't stand upright.

She waited apprehensively for what would come next. Soft leather straps slid over her lower back, and she froze, complete shock coming over her body. When he did nothing more than continue to trail the soft leather over the small of her back and her ass, she slowly let the tension drain from her muscles.

"Do you trust me?" he asked, his tone relaxed, almost lazy.

"Of course I do."

He struck without warning, bringing the straps of the flogger sharply across her ass. Carrie couldn't hold back her yelp of surprise. It stung, but no more than his hand had. It was her emotional reaction that was so different. His hand had been personal. This was not.

He turned the vibe on stronger, pulling his hand back, running the flogger down her ass, tapping it between her thighs.

"Still trust me, baby?" His voice was a dark rasp.

"Yes, I do," she whispered.

She felt his teeth on her neck.

"Liar," he whispered. The flogger hit harder this time, the leather straps curling between her thighs, wedging the vibrator even deeper.

"Who do you trust? Who do you belong to? Who makes you come?"

Marcus kept up the questions and Carrie kept answering him. "You, Marcus, you."

With each question, each answer, he struck her with the flogger. Her ass was hot and her pussy was even hotter. Her thighs were dripping and she had to clench her muscles tightly to keep the vibrator lodged in her.

She was more turned on than she ever had been before but as ecstatic as her body was, her mind was in turmoil. Marcus was pushing her body to the limits, asking her if she trusted him, demanding something more from her than words.

She became confused, and then pissed. What the hell more did he want from her? She begged him to let her come and he refused to give her that release. The generous lover she'd come to expect was nothing but a memory. This lover wanted nothing more than to utterly control her, but rather than doing it for their mutual pleasure, he seemed driven by some dark emotion. His command over her ability to come was raising the stakes.

Then a thought took form in her brain. The Viper had entered this room.

Not in person, but in Marcus' mind. Anger, frustration and desire flooded her as she realized what he was doing. By not letting her come, he was pushing, seeing how much she would take before she broke and walked away from him.

To hell with that! He wasn't going to break her. No man would ever break her. She liked being dominated in the bedroom, yes, but she'd be damned if she was going to put up with another woman in the room. If he needed to exorcise the ghost of Karen, he could do it alone.

She opened her mouth to call out the safe word but images of their time together flashed through her mind. Was she ready to walk away right now because of that woman? Hell no, The Viper was not going to win this time. Instead of uttering the word that would separate them forever, she took a deep breath and let her head fall back.

Marcus had moved back in front of her and was poised on his knees, head bowed as he flicked the ends of the flogger over her pussy, aiming for her swollen clit. She stared down at his glossy black hair. It was so hard to concentrate with him touching her.

She shook her head, trying to clear her brain.

"Marcus, I'm not Karen." She fought hard to keep her voice calm and even. It was ragged and raw from her pleasured screams. He didn't respond, so she repeated herself. Still calm. Still even. "Marcus, Karen is not in this room. I'm not her."

Marcus froze at her softly spoken words. He let the flogger slide to the floor and pressed his forehead to Carrie's belly, clutching at her thighs as he fought raggedly for breath.

Fuck, was that what he was doing? Taking out on Carrie what that bitch had said to him at the restaurant?

All he'd wanted, all he'd needed was to know that Carrie could take all he had to give without breaking. But, goddammit, he'd let that evil woman almost ruin the best thing that ever walked into his life. He tilted his head back and hesitantly met her eyes.

When he saw her face, the sickness in his gut just churned harder. Her lips were red and swollen from her own teeth, and her eyes were wet. Streaks were clearly visible on her cheeks, where tears had overflowed.

"I know you're not her," was all he could manage as he tugged the vibrator from her unresisting sheath. He reached out and unhooked the harness that kept her bent and open for his pleasure. He eased her upright and freed her from the ropes he'd used to restrain her. Wincing when he saw the red marks on her wrists and ankles, he wondered how she would ever forgive or trust him again. He was losing his mind. Marcus never second-guessed himself; now he was.

Once she was loose, she tried to hold him but he wouldn't let her. He had no business accepting comfort from her. She was the one who'd been mistreated. Touching her like the finest crystal, Marcus scooped her into his arms and carried her from the room.

When he reached his bedroom, he settled her gently on the bed, carefully laying her back against the pillows. He sat next to her, holding her face in his palm, and bent to kiss her gently.

"I know you're not her," was all he managed to get out before the guilt choked off his words.

His mouth traveled along her entire face, dusting her cheeks and nose with soft kisses, sipping the tears from her skin. He savored the sweet, silky taste of her, now so familiar and necessary.

He made his way down to her breasts. Damn, he loved them. They were so full and soft and responsive to his lightest touch. Pulling one nipple into his mouth, he loved it with tongue and teeth, drawing sweet moan after moan from his woman. Leaving one breast for the other, he gave it the same careful attention.

One hand cupped the bounty of her breast. The other he trailed down her body until his fingers could slide down on either side of her swollen clit, capturing it in a gentle vise.

"Baby, I want you to come," he said as he pinched her clit lightly.

Her eyes widened and her scream poured into the room. She was amazing, coming with just one word, coming apart beneath him.

When she finally calmed, he reached down to kiss her again. "Damn, baby, I love to watch you come for me."

She smiled at him with the warm glow of a satisfied female. "I love you watching me come," she purred.

Marcus stroked her flushed cheek and bent down, letting his lips linger against hers. He didn't know what he'd done to deserve her, to deserve her easy absolution of his crimes, but he knew he'd take it. Greedy bastard that he was, he'd take everything she gave and demand more.

As his lips toyed with hers, her hands roved restlessly over his back, hooking in the waistband of his pants and tugging at them with clear irritation.

Marcus moved from the bed and quickly skinned out of his jeans and boxer briefs. Stepping to the foot of the bed, he crawled slowly up, parting her legs as he slid up her body.

He paused when his head was level with her pussy, breathing in her sweet, spicy scent. Propping her thighs over his shoulders, he dipped his head and dragged his tongue along the length of her slit, nibbling at sensitive tissues and letting his tongue explore every crevice and fold he encountered.

Carrie arched into his mouth, gasping out his name as he settled in to feast on her needy flesh. Marcus propped himself on his elbows and used his thumbs to open her lips wide. This position gave him total access to her hard little cherry, and he drew it between greedy lips, pulling and sucking until she was sobbing out her pleasure.

When he could sense she was on the edge, struggling to keep her climax at bay, he pulled his mouth slowly off her pussy. He continued crawling up the length of her body, moving her legs until he could nestle between her thighs, settling into the cradle of her hips. Placing his aching cock at the mouth of her opening, he reached down and whisked his thumb over her yearning clit, and whispered against her lips, "Again, baby. Come for me again."

Before he'd even finished speaking, she twisted against him, crying out as the pleasure took her. As soon as he felt her muscles clench, he tunneled into her, reveling in the feel of her coming apart around him, pulling him inside and dragging him along with her. It was beautiful, feeling her body react to his touch. Groaning her name, he ground himself against her, riding out her orgasm with her.

Carrie tangled her hands in his hair and pulled him up until his lips met hers. She kissed him with an intensity he'd never found with anyone else. An intensity that spoke of more than sex. Unable to resist, Marcus sank against her and did something he hadn't done in many, many years.

He made love with Carrie.

Soft touches, softer words. The Dom took his pleasure from hers as he went about worshipping her every curve, her taste, her scent. It was mind-blowing to feel this close to another person. When the passion built and the need became unbearable, only then did Marcus increase his movements, pumping and thrusting, his gaze never leaving her brown eyes.

"I'm here, baby." Her pleasure at his admission was clear in those amazing brown eyes. Her body strained against him. His was like corded steel, every muscle tight, throbbing for release.

"Come with me, baby," he whispered and reveled in the sensation as her sheath clutched down on him, clenching and pulling her name from his throat. Her pleasure caught him in a vise grip and pulled him along with her. Grunting as the pleasure jolted through him, he kissed her, taking her orgasm into himself and pouring his into her.

He loved this woman, loved her so fucking much he felt like he was going to combust.

When the last of their mutual shivers ended, Marcus rolled to his side, pulling her into the cradle of his body, tucked up against him like a spoon.

"Hurricane Marcus," she murmured against his upper arm. He laughed at the wonder in her voice.

She snuggled back into him and he felt her smile against his biceps.

"That was unbelievably amazing." Her voice was fading. "Thank you."

She yawned and he knew that she was exhausted. They would have to talk about what had happened, about Karen, but Marcus was relieved to put it off until later.

"Sleep, baby." He kissed her head again, pulling her tighter against him.

"Love you, Marcus…"

His head came up as her voice trailed off to silence. Carrie was out, breathing deeply. Had he heard her right? Damn, he hoped so, because he felt the exact same way. He had come to a decision, and tomorrow he was telling her that he wasn't letting her go after the weekend was over. In fact, he wasn't letting go of her ever.

A peaceful, relaxed feeling washed over Marcus, and he fell into a deep, restful sleep with a smile on his face.

Chapter Seventeen

&

The music of Shinedown filled the room as her cell phone rang. Carrie shot off the bed like a bullet as the phone kept shrilling, insisting that she answer it.

Snapping the device open, her sleepy eyes barely open, she rasped out an indistinct, "Hello."

"Carrie dear, Cass is in labor."

Carrie came awake instantly and completely at her mother's words. "Oh no," she responded. "It's too early."

"Yes, dear, I know. Now just stay calm." Carrie's mother sounded like she could have stood to follow her own advice. "The baby has decided she's ready to make her appearance. Since this is a first baby, the doctor said it will probably be quite a while before she actually delivers, but she's awfully uncomfortable and she's asking for you."

Carrie winced. As Cassidy's labor coach, she should have been with her from the first contractions.

Her mother continued, "I went ahead and made flight reservations for you. You have an hour and a half before your flight takes off."

Her mother quickly gave her the details of her flight information, and she smiled at the image of her younger sister, ready to bring her baby into the world.

"So, she's asking for me, huh?" Somehow Carrie had a tough time imagining Cassidy doing anything so calm as asking.

Apparently her mom read her mind, because she chuckled. "You better get here now, Care-bear. Cass is screaming for you."

141

"Okay, Mom, see you in a bit." She was still smiling as she hung up the phone. That's when she remembered where she was. Marcus wasn't in the room, and when she went looking for him, he was nowhere to be found.

She felt uneasy. Where was he? She looked at the clock. It was already nine-thirty and her flight left at eleven-fifteen. She had no time to wait around and see when he was coming back. She tried in vain to find a pen or pencil to scribble a message for him. In her frazzled state, she flung her hands up in disgust.

How could he not have a damn pen!

She fought back her anger and sorrow. Damn it, she should have had one more day with him. She quickly dressed in her own clothes, neatly folding the ones he'd purchased for her. There was no way she could keep the items, beautiful as they were. The pain at leaving was already lancing through her heart and she knew that any reminder of the man she loved would only prolong her grieving process.

She would call Marcus from the airport just to let him know that she hadn't walked out on him, and that she would always treasure their time together. Carrie, ever the practical girl, knew that this was the end. In spite of her best intentions, she'd built some dream that Marcus felt more, wanted more than one weekend of sex. She'd known better and the pain was excruciating. She could not stop the tears as she closed the front door and got into her car.

Looking into the rearview mirror at his house, she let the tears flow. How did a person get over finding then losing their soul mate? The one person who totally got them, knew all there was to know about a person, and wanted them warts and all? She swallowed hard, blinking past the tears as her heart cracked then broke wide open.

Marcus jogged up the stone steps to his house, juggling hot coffee in a tray and a bag of bagels. He knew that Carrie would be famished this morning. Their weekend had gone a million times better than Marcus could ever have dreamed, and he knew he'd worn her out.

Damn, but she was an unbelievable woman. He chuckled to himself as he remembered how she'd handled Karen at the restaurant.

A small pang of guilt stabbed at the vicinity of his heart. When they got back home, Carrie had borne the brunt of Marcus' frustration at seeing his ex. He hadn't hurt her, at least not physically, he would never do that, but he'd been rough.

She said she loved it, loved feeling him so deep and hard inside of her. He swore he'd even heard her murmur that she loved *him* as she drifted off to sleep.

Was it true? Could he have gotten so fucking lucky as to have her really love him? God knew she had reached in and grabbed him, twisting his insides out until he was helplessly lost. All she had done was surrender to him. She gave and gave without question. The best part? Outside of the bedroom, she was still the same smart, sassy-mouthed woman whom he'd worked side by side with for so long.

He wanted more. True, two days wasn't a long period of time to make this kind of decision, but Marcus was the kind of man who went after what he wanted with determination.

He knew what he wanted from Carrie. A week, a month, hell a year wouldn't make it any clearer to him than it was right now. He belonged to her and she belonged to him. He loved saying that to himself.

She was his.

Daniel was right. He'd seen through Marcus' denials and bullshit, and Marcus would never be able to thank him enough for sticking his perfect nose into Marcus' business and essentially forcing him to admit to himself how he really felt about her.

And Carrie. How would he ever repay her for accepting his offer? For giving him the one thing in life he wanted — acceptance, total acceptance for the man he was.

After setting breakfast on the counter, he bounded up the stairs to his room. He was hot, hard and ready for her again. He hadn't fucked so many times in two days since he was a teenager. He was insatiable with her, and Carrie welcomed him each and every time he reached for her.

"Wake up, baby, you need to eat," he said as he pushed his door open. The bed was empty. Still smiling with wicked anticipation, he checked the bathroom. She wasn't there either.

The hair on the back of his neck rose as a pit opened up in his stomach. He quickly checked the rest of his house. Still no Carrie. Going over to his kitchen window, he peered out. Her car was gone as well.

Where the hell was she?

His phone rang. He sighed as he recognized her number.

"Baby, where are you?" he asked with crushing relief.

There was a sharp crackle.

"Marcus, I'm so sorry…"

"What? Carrie, I can't hear you." His panic rose sharply at her next words, which were broken up by loud crackles of static and abrupt lulls of silence.

"I'm sorry, Marcus… I can't… I have to go now… Bye."

The phone went dead. He immediately dialed her number. A recording came on and informed him the cellular customer he was trying to reach was unavailable.

Running back to his room, he searched. All the clothes he'd purchased for her were folded neatly at the foot of the bed. Her small overnight bag was gone.

He picked up the phone and dialed her house. When her voicemail picked up, he hung up.

He sat on the bed. The scent of their lovemaking surrounded him, tickling his nose. She was gone.

Marcus stood. Well, he wasn't going to make this easy for her. If she wanted out, she'd have to tell him to his face. He may have started this but she damn well wasn't going to finish it.

* * * * *

He arrived at her apartment in record time. Pulling in next to her crookedly parked car, he became really concerned. He ran up to her second floor apartment and started banging on the door.

No answer.

Marcus stopped hammering on the door and leaned in, listening intently for a shower or radio, for anything to let him know she was in there and okay.

After about five minutes of steady pounding, there was still no answer.

What the hell? She could be lying in there hurt or fucking worse.

"Carrie, dammit baby, open the door. We can talk about this. Just let me know you're okay."

Still no answer.

Now he banged harder as his voice rose. "Carrie Anderson, open this fucking door right now!"

From behind, he was suddenly whacked on the shoulder. Furious, Marcus turned around to face his attacker. He had to look down to find her. Way down. The little white-haired woman who stood glaring at him, tapping her foot and clutching a rolled-up newspaper in one hand while the other was propped on her slim hip, had to be at least eighty years old.

"Young man, do you have any clue what time it is?"

Marcus had no response. Being reprimanded by such a tiny female caught him completely off guard.

"She's not home. Came back a while ago. Grabbed a suitcase and got into a taxi. She seemed really upset. Don't suppose you know what all that's about?" She crossed her bony arms and glared at him.

Marcus leaned into the cheap wooden door. He closed his eyes and ran his fingers through his tangled black hair. Mumbling his apologies to the old lady, he started down the stairs.

The old lady's voice followed him. "If this is how you treat her, no wonder she took off."

Marcus didn't give her the opportunity to say more.

The drive home was bad enough but when he reentered the house, his misery only increased. Everywhere he looked, he saw her ghost.

He moved to the kitchen but it just felt empty and alone without her presence.

"Goddammit," he bellowed, sweeping his arm wide. Their breakfast, caught in his swing, flew off the counter and across the kitchen, leaving sprays of coffee dripping down the walls, and bagels scattered across the floor like rocks.

He wanted to punch something, hurt something as much as the pain ripping through his body hurt him. He crossed the room toward the small table that sat in the corner. The flowers he'd bought for her still stood in their crystal vase. He picked up the vase and threw it hard into the wall. He watched the glass shatter and splinter into a thousand pieces.

"Just like my fucking heart!" he screamed to the empty house. This was not how it was supposed to end. God, he had thought what they shared was special, that once-in-a-lifetime kind of shit you saw in movies.

Was he the only one who felt that way? Damn, he'd been so sure that she was feeling that way too.

Did she wake up this morning and wonder if she was in over her head? Except for the static-filled phone call, she'd said nothing else. No note, nothing but her nosy neighbor informing him that Carrie had taken off with a suitcase and seemed upset.

God, he was such a fool. What woman in her right mind would put up with his shit? A couple nights of play were one thing. A whole lifetime was something completely different. She'd run, he feared, because she was afraid that she would have to have sex with him like that every night.

Marcus slid down the wall until he was sitting on the floor, fumbling for the phone in his pocket. Banging his head back against the wall, he glared at the little device before giving in and dialing.

God, he didn't want to talk to Meredith. His nerves were strung tight and he didn't have the patience to handle her with kid gloves this morning.

To add insult to injury, she didn't answer her phone. Marcus glanced at the clock. Coffee was dripping down its face, and the sight just rekindled his anger.

Cursing steadily, he punched in her cell number. No answer there either. Finally, in a towering rage, he settled in to hitting the redial button every time her phone went to voice mail. He was itching to make someone hurt as bad as he did by the time Meredith finally answered the phone.

"Yes, Marcus." She sounded way more relaxed than she had any right to.

"Meredith. Where the fuck are you?" He didn't even try to moderate his tone. He was beyond being careful of Meri's emotions. He was going on pure rage.

"It's ten-fifteen on Sunday morning. I believe you informed me you'd be unreachable all weekend." Her voice held its usual mockery but it somehow sounded softer. Maybe later that would matter to him but for now Marcus was blind to anything but the emotions tearing at him. "I expected you'd be too busy to call."

Her words were like salt in an open wound. He should be too busy to call. He should be balls-deep in his woman right now, not sitting in a pathetic heap on the floor. His anger had nowhere to go but out.

"Stop being such a fucking ice-bitch and listen to me."

"Marcus." If he'd been listening, he would have heard all the tentative softness disappear from her voice. "I know you think you have a good reason to attack me but trust me, big brother, you don't ever want to go there again."

While her tone didn't reach him, her words did. He forced himself to be silent for a moment, struggling for control. When he thought he could speak without screaming, he rasped, "Call Matt and tell him to get his ass into the office tomorrow. I won't be there."

"Tell me what's going on."

He couldn't take it anymore. Carrie was gone. Meredith was questioning him. His control was shot.

"Just tell Matty to get the fuck to work tomorrow." He slammed the phone closed. Seconds later it joined the pieces of broken glass on the floor when Marcus flung it at the wall.

One long hour of pacing and prowling later, he couldn't stand to be in the house a minute longer. Going into his room, he stuffed random clothing into a duffle bag. He was very careful not to look at the bed or Carrie's neatly folded clothing. He wasn't fucking staying here with her scent on his sheets and her face everywhere he looked.

Throwing his car into gear, he sped out of his driveway, heading to the only place where he absolutely knew he could be alone.

He used his key to enter the empty club. Velvet Ice looked so different in the light of day. The dark walls closed around Marcus as he strode through the regular bar and toward the staircase leading to the second and third floors.

"Hey man, what's up?"

Marcus slowed, looking at the top of the stairs. Brady Ryder, the public partner of the bar, leaned casually against the railing.

Marcus climbed the rest of the way up. "I need someplace to crash. No one knows I'm here and it's gonna stay that way. Understand?"

The other man nodded curtly. Marcus knew that Brady wouldn't question him. The tattooed Dom never took part in the club's many pleasures and perversions, just watched silently. Brady Ryder looked like what he was—a man with enough secrets and torment of his own. He didn't need to dip into Marcus'.

Arriving on the third floor, Marcus went to his room and unlocked it. He didn't bother turning on the light, preferring the darkness. He grabbed a drink from behind the small bar in the corner.

He could just hear Meredith now. *Isn't it a little early to have a drink?*

Marcus saluted the air.

"You're right, sis, it *is* a little early to have a drink. But since I plan on more than one, why not get started?"

He tossed back the vodka, grabbing the neck of the bottle before he stalked to the bed.

Yep, he was going to get nice and tanked and feel sorry for himself. It was easier than dwelling on how the best thing that ever happened to him had walked out of his life. He didn't want to think about how he hungered for what they could have together. Marcus wanted the happy ever after, the white picket fence and kids. Fuck, he even wanted a damn dog.

Never in his life had he considered those things for himself. Stirling had made sure that none of his children wanted to produce a Worthington heir. Now Marcus did, and he wanted it with Carrie. She would be the kind of mother who showered her kids with love. She could show Marcus how not to be so hard. With her, he allowed himself to be gentle, to be open and unguarded, all the things a father should be with his children.

He waited for the tears to form but they never did. This was different than when Karen had betrayed him. Karen had wounded his pride. This time he felt utterly empty and alone and he knew that his life was never going to be the same, if he ever recovered at all.

Karen had humiliated the man, his ego was bruised.

Carrie had broken his heart.

* * * * *

Four days later, Marcus sat on the dock, staring out at Silver Lake. He hadn't been able to tolerate being in the club once it opened. The music and sex did nothing except remind him of the last time he'd been there. The night Carrie had invaded his world and turned everything upside down.

He couldn't stay home either. Everywhere he looked, he saw her. In his bed. In the tub. At the fucking kitchen table. She haunted the place.

He thought about work but couldn't find the desire to go there either. For the first time in his life, Marcus Worthington couldn't focus on business. Carrie had stolen his mind when she'd stolen his heart and soul. He wondered if she even knew it.

So he'd spent the last four days at Matthew's vacation cottage. The "Love Shack". The place Matty brought his conquests *du jour*. It was the only place Marcus could think of where he could be alone. Where visions of Carrie wouldn't haunt him.

Of course he'd been deluding himself. He carried her inside, in the place his heart used to be. By Thursday afternoon, Marcus realized that there was nowhere on earth he could go where she wouldn't haunt him.

Finally, heaving a sigh, he bowed to the inevitable. She was gone and, unless he wanted to jump into the lake and drown himself, life would somehow have to go on.

Running a weary hand over his eyes, he rose and headed for his car.

Chapter Eighteen

🔊

Marcus couldn't believe he was doing a drive-by. Again. He'd been reduced to haunting Carrie's apartment building like a ghost and he didn't like how pathetic it made him feel. It was a good thing he did it though. Tonight there was a light in the window. He felt like a stalker as he watched and waited.

A shadow passed in front of the curtains, a female form that he'd know anywhere. Carrie was home! He didn't know what was stronger—his relief that she was home and seemed safe, his anger that she'd left him in the first place or his fear that she wouldn't want to see him. After all, she'd only promised a weekend. But, by God, she owed him one more day and if that's all he could get, he was determined to take it.

He scratched his face; he needed a shave. He smiled a little bit at the vision of her creamy breasts rosy with whisker burn. He wouldn't have chosen to go to her scruffy, but frankly at the moment he really didn't care how he looked. The last four days had been a virtual hell. One he never intended to live again.

The time he'd spent alone had done little to calm his pain or his anger. At first he'd determined to just let her go. It was for the best for both of them. That resolution had lasted all of twenty-four hours. Then memories of her sweetness, her sass, her luscious body had overcome his good sense. He'd known he had to get her back.

He'd even broken down and tried to find her. He'd gone over in his mind every detail he could remember from their conversations. He didn't remember her sister's last name but he had managed to track her parents' number down, only to get an answering machine when he called.

He'd wanted to give up. He almost *had* given up. But the devil on his shoulder and the vision of her liquid brown eyes when she'd told him she wanted to feel him come inside her had him making the three-hour drive from Matt's lake cottage and cruising by Carrie's apartment one more time.

Now, staring up at her window he felt pathetic. Pathetic and pissed. He'd fallen hard and deep for this woman, something he'd vowed never to do again. Now as he pushed open his car door, he knew he was going to her at least this one last time. He had to know why. Why she fucking left with only that one phone call. Why, after what they shared, had she turned away from him with no explanation?

Marcus bounded up the stairs two at a time. His heart was in his throat. He was shaking as he knocked heavily on the door. He waited about ten seconds before, unable to find his legendary patience, he started to knock again. Two apartment doors simultaneously flew open.

His eyes locked on Carrie. She stood there looking so damn good. She was wearing an old terry cloth robe, her wet hair hanging in strings around her shoulders. Her face was bare of makeup, and Marcus thought he'd never seen such a beautiful woman in his entire life. His cock rose to attention and he gave a mental curse. Now was so not the time for that.

"You again."

He cringed as he recognized the old lady from Sunday morning. He shot her a quick glance and was relieved to note that she was not holding a newspaper this time.

"This young man came pounding on your door at an unacceptable hour Sunday morning."

"It was after ten a.m.," Marcus growled.

"Sorry, Mrs. Meyers." Carrie laughed. The old woman sniffed and closed her door.

"Well, are you going to just stand there?" she asked.

Marc drank in the sight of her, forgetting for a moment that he was pissed. "I think I should."

Her full bottom lip tilted down in confusion. "Ok, but do you really want Mrs. Meyers to hear what you have to say?"

He definitely did not want that old crow knowing his business.

He moved forward into the apartment and shut the door but would not come any farther into her home.

"Marcus, what's wrong?" She looked so genuinely confused that Marcus saw red.

"What's *wrong*?" He knew he was yelling but he couldn't seem to help it. "What the hell kind of question is that? I'm a little disappointed, baby. For such a smart woman, you're being awfully obtuse."

Carrie knitted her eyebrows together at his insult. This sure as hell wasn't the welcome home she expected. He was angry, apparently at her.

"Marcus, I think you need to explain what the hell is wrong with you." She didn't even try to keep the bite out of her voice.

"Oh, I don't know… How about the fact that the woman I love walked out on me without a word?"

"But, Marcus…" Wait. Did he just say the "L" word?

"No. Just stop right there. I've been waiting for four fucking days!" He was yelling again. "Was it really so bad?" he asked, stepping up to her, his mouth a scant inch from her lips. "Damn, baby, you sure had me fooled. You'll have to forgive me for thinking you liked it, the way your body responded to *everything* I did to you."

Carrie wasn't sure if she wanted to smack him or kiss the sneer off his face. At the same time, her confusion only grew more. He strode past her and into her small living room.

"I was actually going to come up here and tell you that I would go vanilla for you. That I'd decided if you hated what I wanted so much, I would change for you." His face was flinty, expressionless as he continued. "I didn't mean to hurt you or to scare you. I would never deliberately hurt you." Only his disheveled appearance and the dark circles under his eyes gave away his torment.

He walked past her again. She reached for him but he jerked away from her before she could touch him. She felt like she'd fallen into an episode of *The Twilight Zone*.

"But I can't be someone else, not even for the woman I love." His voice caught on the word *love*.

He wouldn't let her near him, so out of desperation she did the only thing she could think of to catch his attention.

"Marcus Aaron Worthington, you're a bastard." Her angry voice stopped him in his tracks. He turned to her, his face red with fury.

She dropped the robe, crossed her wrists behind her head and stood there. A wicked grin spread across her face as Marcus' eyes flashed silver.

"Now that I have your attention, why don't you explain to me what *the hell* is wrong with you." She took a tentative step closer to him. He backed up until his back hit the door, and she rolled her eyes. "Obviously we have gotten our wires crossed."

"You left me." His voice sounded almost broken, a sound she would never have expected from him.

"What are you talking about? I didn't *leave* you. I went *to* my sister. Cassidy went into labor early and I had to get to her as fast as possible. I did, in fact, call you and tell you just that."

The color drained from his face. He went white and seemed to collapse against the door.

"Besides," she continued, "when I woke up, you were gone. Nowhere to be found. I had to run in order to catch the next flight to Chicago and I had no way of contacting you." She sent him a pointed look. "You didn't have your cell phone with you."

When Marcus finally responded, it was slowly, as if each word was being dragged out of him.

"I only heard you say that you couldn't do this, and then goodbye." He closed his eyes and tipped his head back against the door. "I thought I'd asked too much of you. That I'd hurt you or scared you. That I'd driven you away forever."

Marcus looked so lost that Carrie almost wanted to take pity on him. Almost. But she knew that her man needed a firm hand, so she stalked up to him, crowding him against the door until she could feel his heat seeping into her naked flesh.

"You know, Marcus," she gave him back his own words. "For a smart man, you're acting like an ass. A wonderful, sexy, arrogant ass." One slender finger poked into his chest with each word. "Even after all we shared, you didn't give me the slightest hint you wanted anything more than one weekend. How was I supposed to know? It should be me screaming my lungs out."

Her palms moved to his chest, which was still heaving with emotion. She smoothed his shirt before beginning to unbutton it.

"I tried calling several times this week and you were nowhere to be found." Her fingers tiptoed over his hot skin and she hummed her enjoyment, leaning forward to lick at one hard, male nipple.

Drawing back a little, she cupped her breasts, offering them to his famished gaze. "And tell me, how many women would do this if they were running from you?"

Marcus felt dizzy as he watched her walk backward and kneel on the carpet, taking her position, red velvet collar circling her delicate throat, presenting him with her newly pierced nipples. All the blood rushed from his head to his dick.

Christ! He *was* an ass. A stupid one, too. The whole time he'd been brooding at Matty's party cabin, she'd been in Chicago. Carrie hadn't left him. *Carrie hadn't left him!* He brought one hand up to his mouth as his eyes devoured the ornaments dangling from those cherry-red nipples.

"God, baby, do they hurt?"

"Oh, yes they do. The girl said they were going be sore for a while. You'll just have to be extra careful with them." Her brown eyes fluttered as she answered.

"So are you going to stand there all day and just stare at me?" she asked.

He felt his eyes darken at her sassy attitude. Before she could do more than widen her eyes at him, Marcus pounced on her, pushing her back into the carpet and following her in a rush that stole her breath.

Marcus bit into Carrie's neck as he whispered, "God, baby, I thought I'd lost you."

He felt her shudder against him. "Marcus, I thought you only wanted a weekend. And then, after seeing her…"

"Shhh… not now… Soon, but not now. Now I need to be inside of you."

He clumsily ripped open his jeans, managing to pull them down enough to free his dick and guide the wet head into her entrance.

He thrust home and they both cried out. His mouth trailed a path down her neck and traced hot, damp circles over her breasts, homing in on her waiting nipples. When he carefully licked the pierced buds, Carrie hissed, but when he went to remove his mouth she held the back of his head, keeping him in place.

He couldn't go hard, so he gently pulled the small golden ring into his mouth, flicking his tongue against the very tip of her nipple. She arched hard against him, grinding her clit into his pubic bone and thrusting her nipple farther into his mouth. He sucked the neglected nipple between his lips, taking his time and making sure his movements were slow and easy.

Carrie's eyes were dazed as she wrapped her thighs around his ass. "Please, Marcus," she begged incoherently.

He levered himself up a little, grabbing her hands and placing them over her head. Holding her wrists in one hand, he pumped inside of her. He was raised enough so that his chest didn't rub her newly pierced nipples but he loved the picture they made swaying as he drove into her over and over again.

His mouth clamped down on hers in a kiss so scorching that, by the time he came up for air, her lips were swollen and red. God, she was so fucking gorgeous and she was his.

Changing his angle, he let go of her and pushed up to his knees. Folding her thighs back, he muttered, "Watch, baby. Watch me move in you. Fuck, you're so creamy for me. Look, it's all over my cock."

She stared at the place where they were joined, her eyes going wide with the wonder of their lovemaking. Marcus placed his finger on her tight little button, rubbing and teasing her to the brink of orgasm over and over until tears formed at the corners of her eyes.

Just when she knew she couldn't take one more second of his torture, he slowed even more until time stretched like hot taffy and it seemed like he'd been loving her forever, would keep loving her forever.

Nothing had ever been as perfect as this moment. There were no flowers, no silk sheets, none of the trappings of romance. Looking into her eyes, Marcus saw everything he ever needed. She was his, forever. She craved him, just as he was, the way he craved her. Unable to stave off the emotion filling him up, he buried his face in her neck, swallowing back the first tears he'd let fall in five years.

But these were tears of happiness. A kind of happiness that Marcus never dreamed existed between two people. He sounded like a sappy ass, and for once he didn't give a damn. For Carrie, he was willing to be anything she wanted, anything she needed. And the best part was that she needed him to dominate her in the bedroom. She needed him to love her every day and night.

"Come with me, baby," he whispered into her ear. She tightened around him and sobbed his name as her release rippled over him, clenching him in a velvet fist. It was too much for him and he let loose, pumping his love and his seed into her sweet recesses.

He managed to roll his weight off of her, going to her side and tucking her against him.

"Now, what was all that business about loving me?" She was giving him a naughty, cheeky smile, and he let his hand drift down her back before smacking her soundly on the butt. When she pouted at him, he relented. Gazing into her eyes, he gave her his soul.

"I love you, Carrie Anderson." It was short and sweet and not very romantic, but it was everything.

Tears welled in her brown eyes. He wiped them gently with his thumbs.

"I love you, Marcus Worthington." Her voice and her smile trembled. All the love in the world was shining in her eyes and it took his breath away. "I always have, always will."

He dipped his head and kissed her, long and lingering. He savored the taste of his woman, realizing all over again how much he'd missed her these past few days.

"How does October sound?" he eventually murmured as he nuzzled her throat.

"How does it sound for what?" She moved her head to the side, allowing him greater access to the sensitive skin there.

"For our wedding, baby. You don't think I'm going to let you go now, do you?"

Her breath caught and she leaned up to kiss his lips.

"Well, since you put it that way, I suppose I could pencil it in."

He stopped his nibbling and gazed down at her as he rested on his elbows. She lay naked and fragile-seeming under his nearly clothed body, and she was his. He wanted to scream it from the rooftops but for now he would settle for hearing Carrie scream his name.

"Thank you, baby."

"For what?"

He watched her pale face blush.

"For bringing me back to life." It was all he managed to get out before sliding back into her, into his home.

Carrie brought her hands down around him and held on for dear life as the pleasure he created in her took flight. He drove slowly into her pussy. She drank in his every tremble, absorbing all the emotion he couldn't say with words.

Her pussy contracted as her orgasm came out of nowhere. Her hips lifted off the floor as she clasped him desperately inside of her. Marcus flung his head back, his veins popping out on his neck. He screamed her name as he came inside of her.

Mrs. Meyers would have plenty to tell the neighbors now.

Epilogue

৪০

Carrie escaped into her dressing room, ready to relax and have a few moments to herself. She loved her mother and sister but they were driving her nuts with all their hovering.

She headed toward the antique white table that held a large mirror for her to apply her makeup. Marcus had offered to bring in a makeup artist but Carrie had refused. It was a little daunting to suddenly be wealthy enough to afford most anything. She was a prudent girl and couldn't justify the extravagance.

Sitting in the middle of the table was a plain black box. A smile lit her face. Marcus always gave her gifts in a black box. She slid the red bow off and threw the lid to the floor.

Inside laid a red silk scarf. Next to that was a box from Marcus' favorite jeweler. Carrie lifted the velvet container and raised the lid.

"Oh my," she exclaimed as her fingers brushed over the jewel-encrusted collar and nipple rings. They matched the diamond-and-ruby engagement ring Marcus had given her.

The last thing in the box was a note written in bold black ink. *Put the new rings on for me Carrie, then the blindfold, and present yourself for me.*

She was reaching for the scarf when the door swung open.

"Honey, do you need anything?" Her mother bustled into the room and up to the table. Spotting the jewelry box, she cried out when she saw the gems. "Oh, Carrie, what beautiful earrings." She closed the lid. "Marcus sure is going to spoil my girl."

Carrie's face burned with embarrassment and she stifled a giggle. *Earrings.*

"Mom, I could really use some time alone." She wrapped an arm around her mother's waist, hugging her tightly while trying not to seem too eager to push the woman out of the room.

"Of course, dear." Her mom bent over and kissed her cheek. "I remember getting ready for my wedding to your father." The older woman sighed blissfully. "All my mother wanted to do was hover like a mama hen and all I wanted to do was sit and daydream about my wedding night." Her mom looked down at Carrie and blushed a little bit, then gave a naughty smile. "Now, do we have to have a talk about what you should expect on your wedding night?"

Carrie sputtered with laughter. Her mom had no idea what her wedding night would be like. Her mother joined in with her laughter and the two women shared a long moment of affection and joy until, with a final kiss on the cheek, she left her alone. Carrie turned back to the mirror and watched her mother's reflection leave.

Carefully, she removed the simple gold hoops that had adorned her breasts and replaced them with the diamond-and-ruby ones. The weight of the gems felt delicious. She knelt on the floor in only her white lace panties. Tying the blindfold tightly over her eyes, she waited for Marcus to come to her.

She heard the lock click into place, felt his presence in the small room.

"You know it's bad luck to see the bride on your wedding day." Her breath caught in her throat as she felt him standing behind her. Not touching her, just letting his body heat seep into her skin.

"I don't see you, at least not all of you." His voice was lazy and deep, a sure sign he wanted something. "I have to have your taste on my tongue as you walk down the aisle, baby. Besides, I wanted to know if you liked your gifts."

"They're beautiful." She laughed again. "My mother saw them and thought they were earrings." Her laughter trailed off as she felt the collar rub against the back of her neck.

"Mmm. Well, I suppose it's a good thing she doesn't know how naughty her daughter really is." His voice was full of contented amusement and his breath brushed her ear as he knelt down behind her. His hands landed lightly on her shoulders, and his tone turned serious.

"Baby, will you wear my collar? Once I put it on you, you're mine, forever."

"Oh, God yes, Marcus. I will wear it always. Besides, I'm already yours forever."

He rewarded her with a single kiss to the side of her neck and clasped the collar into place. He rose.

"Here," he said. "I want you on your feet." He helped her into a standing position and led her to one side of the room.

"Bend over for me, baby," Marcus commanded. Carrie bent at the waist and her chest hit the back of a velvet chair. "Hands behind your back."

Excitement caused her pussy to heat and liquid to seep between her thighs as she brought her hands behind her, lacing her fingers together. She sighed as she felt the familiar bindings lacing up from her wrists and ending at her elbows.

He gently lifted her by her arms, guiding her to sit on the chair.

"Baby, you look so good," he whispered as his hands slid up and down her bare legs. He grabbed a foot and rolled on one delicate silk stocking, securing it to her lacy garter belt. Working slowly, he repeated the process on her other leg.

"I have another gift for you," he murmured.

Carrie's body shook with anticipation. She knew now exactly what he was capable of, what they were capable of together. Her lover was insatiable. He hadn't given her a moment's peace since they'd become engaged. Not that she was complaining. She loved every bit of the time they spent together.

He nibbled at her shoulders, soothing the marks he left with a slow sweep of his tongue.

She let her head fall back and whispered in a shaky voice, "Remember, strapless gown."

Marcus growled but moved his attention lower.

She felt the familiar cool kiss of the lube as he rubbed it along her ass, piercing the tight hole hiding there.

When he had her completely ready for him, Marcus kissed her fully on the lips. "Push down for me, baby."

Carrie pushed her ass down, feeling the burning, and maddening pressure. He slid the slim plug in all the way. It wasn't uncomfortable but she could definitely feel it. Marcus lifted each of her legs and laid them over the arms of the chair.

"Spread those legs wide for me, baby."

Her head fell forward as strong, warm fingers dug into the top of her thighs, opening her up to his firm mouth.

God, she was beautiful, Marcus thought as he wiggled his tongue between her plump labia. She was so wet for him. He loved that about her. Carrie was always ready to take him. Hell, no woman had ever kept him so satisfied and so horny all at the same time. He hadn't thought it possible.

He blew a heated breath between her thighs and she stifled a moan. He liked that throttled sound and went to work to get more. He pushed his fingers along her slit until he found her sweet little clit. Wrapping his lips around it, he suckled it into his mouth.

He would love to buy her still another ring to match her collar, this one attached to her clit. Of course, when he'd made that suggestion she had countered that he should get himself pierced for her as well. He wanted to laugh, because he had rushed out last night to do just that. Sure, it was just one nipple, but hell, it was a start. He'd put a hole through his dick if it would make her happy.

Marcus knew Carrie would get a kick out of playing with his sore chest. She would make him pay for the fact that he hadn't been able to keep his mouth or fingers away from her nipples as they'd healed.

Smiling wickedly at the thought, he slipped two fingers into her wet passage, sliding up, up, up and back down, timing the thrust of his fingers with the rhythm of his tongue. He knew when Carrie was close, he heard her choked whimpers, felt her legs shake, her body ready to give him her orgasm.

Abruptly he pulled back, and with one unsteady hand he unzipped his pants and pulled out his cock. Setting it against her slit, he plowed into her with one long, sure stroke. They moaned in unison as he grabbed each breast. His fingers and thumbs clamped onto her nipple rings, manipulating them to give his woman the greatest pleasure possible. They'd both been overjoyed when her piercings had healed enough to allow Marcus to play with them a little more roughly. A day didn't go by when he hadn't sucked each delightful ring until she was climbing his body, begging him to come inside of her.

She was a match for him in every way. He loved this woman more than life itself and was going to spend the rest of his life proving that fact to her over and over again.

Carrie arched her hips farther, matching him thrust for thrust. Marcus didn't hold back. He let go of one breast and slid eager fingers down to her hood. Diving beneath it, he rubbed and slid around the sensitive tissue until Carrie was begging.

"Marcus, please, I need to come. I can't hold back."

"Then come for me, baby." The familiar words tore raggedly from him as he bucked into her hard enough to push her to the back of the chair. Her thighs tensed, as did her pussy. Marcus bit down on her shoulder hard as he filled her up with his essence.

Eventually their hearts slowed. He pulled out, stuffing his still-swollen cock back into his tuxedo pants. He didn't want to leave her but getting her down the aisle took precedence over his greedy cock. He helped her to stand and untied her. Completing the familiar ritual, he rubbed away any traces of the silk rope.

"I have one more present for you." He stopped her before she could remove the blindfold. "Wait until I'm gone to take this off." She heard a slight rustle and then he was cupping her cheek in his palm for one last kiss.

"See you in there, baby."

"Ah, Marcus, aren't you forgetting something?" She shook her ass in his direction.

He laughed and kissed her cheek. "Nope. Not forgetting anything at all."

The door had barely latched behind him when she pulled off the silk scarf. There, propped against the mirror, was the painting she'd admired that first weekend they'd spent together. Tucked into one corner of the brushed gold frame was a note.

Without you I am incomplete. From today until forever, I promise to give you this: unconditional love, and as much joy as your heart can hold. Marcus

Carrie felt her eyes overflow and was grateful that she hadn't yet done her makeup.

* * * * *

The ceremony was stunning in its simplicity. Carrie held tightly to Marcus' hands as they were pronounced man and wife and blinked away tears at the sheer devotion she saw in his eyes. As his mouth touched hers, sealing their bargain for eternity, she felt a small vibration coming from the forgotten plug. Marcus swallowed her surprised moan, and when they broke the kiss, he laughed.

Carrie gave him a brilliant smile of her own. He was a dead man. When she finally had him alone tonight, he was going to pay dearly for this little surprise. From the moment she'd opened her first present until now, he had teased and tortured her until she wanted nothing more than to find the nearest closet and push Marcus to the floor. His evil grin told her he knew exactly what she was thinking and wouldn't mind it at all.

He wrapped his arm around her waist as he led her back down the aisle. They still had hours' worth of reception and pictures to get through before she could have her way with him. But she knew he was more than worth the wait.

* * * * *

In the limo, Marcus dragged his new wife onto his lap. The day couldn't have been any more perfect. He'd seen his sister, his Meri, come back to the land of the living. He hoped she'd always find happiness in the arms of her dashing Italian. Matty was healthy and in once piece, seeming whole and recovered from his accident, and Marcus had even sensed some strong vibes bouncing around between Matt and his girlfriend Shannon and *Daniel*, strange as it seemed. But the most perfect part of all was sitting in his lap, her arms circling his neck as he cupped her breast.

"Have I told you how beautiful you are today, Mrs. Worthington?"

"Worthington? Marcus, what makes you think I'm taking your name?"

Marcus rolled her underneath him. Her satin dress slithered easily up her body, giving him immediate and complete access to her sweetness. Marcus freed himself and drove into Carrie, filling her in one hard thrust. Her legs widened and she held him tightly to her.

"This," he growled, driving his hips forward. "This proves you belong to me, Carrie. You wear my collar and my ring, and you'll wear my name too. The world will always know whose woman you are."

Slowly, he lowered his mouth to hers. His lips seared hers with the knowledge that he loved her, that he was owned by her as much as she was by him. As he loved his woman, his wife, Marcus remembered that first day, the deal he'd offered her, and he knew that he had been changed forever by Carrie's answer.

The End

Also by Sierra Summers

න

eBooks:

Conference with the Boss

Corporate Affairs 1: Carrie's Answer *(with VJ Summers)*

Corporate Affairs 2: Meredith's Awakening *(with VJ Summers)*

Longfellow Seduced *(with VJ Summers)*

Finn's Redemption

About the Author

න

Sierra Summers lives in the Metro-Detroit area in Michigan. She is a married mother of two wonderful boys and one precious girl. She also cares for two spoiled dogs.

She still has the first book she ever wrote in first grade, *Skeleton Rock*, which started off her love for writing and she's written ever since. The majority of her books take place in Michigan and she's proud to live so close to Detroit, a city poised on the brink of a comeback. The revitalized downtown and surrounding area provides wonderful inspiration for her writing.

Finding her writing partner, VJ Summers, was the answer to her lifelong dream. Together the duo had written several books before Sierra also began venturing out on her own. Sierra and VJ both love to hear from their readers.

About the Author

മ

When not working the EDJfH (Evil Day Job from Hell), obsessing over whether her parents are getting enough to eat, obsessing that her kid is sexting the boyfriend, making coffee, drinking coffee or feeding the two cats who allow her to live with them, VJ can be found reading or writing erotic romance—either solo as m/m author VJ Summers, or as the shorter, more quiet half of the "Violet Summers" writing team (the tall half is Sierra Summers).

മ

The authors welcome comments from readers. You can find their website and email address on their author bio page at www.ellorascave.com.

Tell Us What You Think

We appreciate hearing reader opinions about our books. You can email us at Comments@EllorasCave.com.

Why an electronic book?

We live in the Information Age—an exciting time in the history of human civilization, in which technology rules supreme and continues to progress in leaps and bounds every minute of every day. For a multitude of reasons, more and more avid literary fans are opting to purchase e-books instead of paper books. The question from those not yet initiated into the world of electronic reading is simply: *Why?*

1. *Price.* An electronic title at Ellora's Cave Publishing runs anywhere from 40% to 75% less than the cover price of the exact same title in paperback format. Why? Basic mathematics and cost. It is less expensive to publish an e-book (no paper and printing, no warehousing and shipping) than it is to publish a paperback, so the savings are passed along to the consumer.

2. *Space.* Running out of room in your house for your books? That is one worry you will never have with electronic books. For a low one-time cost, you can purchase a handheld device specifically designed for e-reading. Many e-readers have large, convenient screens for viewing. Better yet, hundreds of titles can be stored within your new library—on a single microchip. There are a variety of e-readers from different manufacturers. You can also read e-books on your PC or laptop computer. (Please note that Ellora's Cave does not endorse any specific brands.

You can check our website at www.ellorascave.com for information we make available to new consumers.)

3. *Mobility.* Because your new e-library consists of only a microchip within a small, easily transportable e-reader, your entire cache of books can be taken with you wherever you go.

4. *Personal Viewing Preferences.* Are the words you are currently reading too small? Too large? Too… ANNOYING? Paperback books cannot be modified according to personal preferences, but e-books can.

5. *Instant Gratification.* Is it the middle of the night and all the bookstores near you are closed? Are you tired of waiting days, sometimes weeks, for bookstores to ship the novels you bought? Ellora's Cave Publishing sells instantaneous downloads twenty-four hours a day, seven days a week, every day of the year. Our webstore is never closed. Our e-book delivery system is 100% automated, meaning your order is filled as soon as you pay for it.

Those are a few of the top reasons why electronic books are replacing paperbacks for many avid readers.

As always, Ellora's Cave welcomes your questions and comments. We invite you to email us at Comments@ellorascave.com or write to us directly at Ellora's Cave Publishing Inc., 1056 Home Avenue, Akron, OH 44310-3502.

MAKE EACH DAY MORE EXCITING WITH OUR
ELLORA'S
CAVEMEN
CALENDAR
WWW.ELLORASCAVE.COM

ELLORA'S CAVE
Romanticon

Annual convention
for women who
refuse to behave

Made in the USA
Lexington, KY
22 June 2014